ERIB
8/11

SWIM TO WIN

D0973942

SWIM TO WIN

Vallery Hyduk

James Lorimer & Company Ltd., Publishers
Toronto

Copyright © 2011 by Vallery Hyduk

All rights reserved. No part of this book may be reproduced or transmitted in any form or by any means, electronic or mechanical, including photocopying, or by any information storage or retrieval system, without permission in writing from the publisher.

James Lorimer & Company Ltd., Publishers acknowledges the support of the Ontario Arts Council. We acknowledge the financial support of the Government of Canada through the Canada Book Fund for our publishing activities. We acknowledge the support of the Canada Council for the Arts for our publishing program. We acknowledge the Government of Ontario through the Ontario Media Development Corporation's Ontario Book Initiative.

Cover Image: iStockphoto

Library and Archives Canada Cataloguing in Publication

Hyduk, Vallery
     Swim to win / Vallery Hyduk.

(Sports stories)
Issued also in an electronic format.
ISBN 978-1-55277-698-8 (bound).—ISBN 978-1-55277-666-7 (pbk.)

    I. Title. II. Series: Sports stories (Toronto, Ont.)

PS8615.Y48S85 2011   jC813'.6   C2010-907391-6

James Lorimer & Company Ltd.,
Publishers
317 Adelaide Street West
Suite #1002
Toronto, ON, Canada
M5V 1P9
www.lorimer.ca

Distributed in the United States by:
Orca Book Publishers
P.O. Box 468
Custer, WA USA
98240-0468

Printed and bound in Canada.
Manufactured by Webcom in Toronto,
Ontario, Canada in February, 2011.
Job # 375123

MIX
Paper from
responsible sources
FSC® C004071

In memory of William Hyduk, who was my biggest fan.

CONTENTS

1 THE NEW COACH

"I wonder if the fees will go up," said Lasha Boyko's father as they drove to the Birch Hill Community Centre. That was where Lasha trained every day — sometimes even twice a day — as a competitive swimmer.

Lasha sat quietly in the back seat of the minivan, gazing out the window. She liked looking at the big houses that lined the streets leading to Birch Hill, where her schoolmates and many swimmers on her team lived.

"I heard she's getting almost double what good old George got," added Lasha's mom. George had been Lasha's coach since she'd started swimming seriously four years ago. He'd been the Yorktown Swim Club's head coach as long as anyone could remember.

"I think she's making more than you and me combined!" said Lasha's dad.

"Really?" said Lasha.

Her mom suddenly sounded worried. "Geez, you're right. I sure hope they don't increase the fees too much."

Lasha wondered how one person could earn more

than both her parents. Her mom and dad worked so hard that they came home from work every day exhausted.

Home — that's where Lasha should be right now, getting ready for her first day of grade eight tomorrow. But there was no way that she was going to pass up the chance to peek in on tonight's Parents Meeting. It was the first introduction to her swim team's new head coach, Alexia Romanoff.

"I wonder what she'll look like," said Lasha's mom, popping a loose hairpin back into her hair.

"Doesn't matter to me, as long as she does what the club's paying her all these big bucks to do," replied her dad.

"I know it's probably wrong," giggled Lasha's mom. "But I imagine her to be hulking and manly, with a slight moustache."

"Well, she had better not offer our little girl any steroids."

"No. You don't really think that would happen here, do you?"

"You guys! I'd never take steroids!" Lasha couldn't hide her surprise. "That would be cheating!"

"I hate to tell you, sweetie, but your new coach comes from the old Soviet Union. She was a champion athlete back when their athletes were all doped up. They wanted to win at all costs," explained Lasha's dad.

Lasha didn't want to believe any of it. She wanted the new coach to be perfect.

"We'd like to see you win too, but not at *any* cost," said her mom as they pulled into the parking lot. "Besides, I'm sure the club wouldn't hire anyone who would try to hurt our children."

★ ★ ★

Most of the parents in the Birch Hill Community Centre meeting room were good friends. They had spent many years sitting together and chatting through the long practices and the even longer swim meets.

Lasha was the only swimmer in the building when the doors closed to start the meeting. Not content to wait outside while the grown-ups talked, Lasha peered in through the crack in the doors. The only people in the room that she didn't know were a middle-aged woman and a blond-haired man. The woman had short, slicked-back black hair. She towered over the man next to her. Lasha's dad had heard through the swimming grape-vine that the new coach was "built strong, like a dump truck." From this fitting description of the woman, Lasha guessed that she was their new coach. The man, Lasha figured, must be the new assistant coach.

"Could I have everyone's attention?" said Jerry, the mild-mannered club president, rising to the front of the room to begin the meeting.

"As you all know, today is the start of . . . well, it's a new start for the Yorktown Swim Club. This year we made good use of your hard-earned registration fees and the bingo revenue. We're using the money to . . . um . . . up the ante, as they say. We've invested in a new coach that we believe will take the Yorktown swimmers to a new level of success.

"The new coach . . . well, it's no secret anymore . . . her name is Alexia Romanoff. She's had great success in her own swimming career — an Olympic gold medal on her resumé. Not too shabby. She also has seen a lot of success in getting swimmers to the Olympic level *and* onto the Olympic podium. Well, let's see . . ." Jerry paused a moment to check his cue cards. "Since she began coaching outside Russia twenty years ago, she has coached forty-five athletes to the Olympics, mostly in the United States. This is her first time coaching in Canada. So welcome, eh?" Jerry beamed over at the new coach, who remained stone-faced.

"Um . . . wow . . . forty-five Olympians." Jerry looked back at the parents. "Can you believe that? And eight of those swimmers actually won medals, too." He paused to allow for the crowd's reaction.

As the crowd *oohed* and *aahed*, Lasha glanced over at her mom and dad. Her dad's eyes were lit up and her mom was leaning forward in her seat. From the looks on their faces, Lasha could tell they were picturing their daughter as the coach's next Olympic star. But that was an impossible dream. Wasn't it?

In her heart, Lasha was wishing for the same thing.

"Yeah, wow is right! Anyhoo, her reputation certainly precedes her." Jerry's voice brought Lasha's attention back to the meeting. "So without further ado, it is my honour to present the Yorktown Swim Club's new head coach, Alexia Romanoff!"

Alexia Romanoff barely cracked a smile as she was welcomed by a healthy round of applause. Instead, she raised a hand for silence. Then she barked, "This town needs a competition pool! It's crazy to think that a swimmer can have proper training in a pool with a waterslide! This is a leisure pool. We're not here for leisure, are we?"

No one moved. Lasha held her breath.

"This town needs a fifty-metre pool. First thing tomorrow I will start lobbying the mayor's office for new facilities. Each and every one of you should do the same."

Slowly, parents in the audience began to nod in agreement, including Lasha's dad.

"Now," continued Alexia, "I've been hired to do one thing — to take this club to a higher level by making your kids faster swimmers. Yes? You want me to raise the Yorktown Swim Club from mediocrity? You want this club to compete at the national level. Correct?"

Lasha cringed. She didn't like the sound of that word, "mediocrity." She thought she was a pretty good swimmer already. She had a corkboard at home filled with first-place ribbons from the races she'd won.

"What you ask *is* possible. I *can* make it happen. But the question is, can *you* do what it takes to make it happen? Getting to the top takes support. I need the support of all parents. And of course I need hard, HARD work from your children. It will mean harder work than they've ever done in their lives. Do you understand?"

Lasha's heart was pounding. Alexia seemed so scary compared to George.

"One thing I want to be perfectly clear is that I am not here to babysit. If you want a fun place for your kids to go after school, find another program. I don't know what you've been doing, but as of today this club is not offering swimming as a leisure activity. No, this is now a highly COMPETITIVE swim team. I've been a coach for a long time. I also swam for long time. So, trust me, I know how to make great swimmers. Here is my promise to you and your children . . ."

Lasha pushed the door open a bit to hear better.

"If you and your child are willing to put in the time and effort and do exactly what I say, when I say it, both in and out of the pool, then I promise that your child can go to the next level in swimming. All I need is for everyone to know how to say '*yes I can*' and '*yes I will*.'"

The coach scanned the room. Through the crack between the doors, her eyes met Lasha's. Lasha froze. Alexia's lips formed a half smile and she gave her a look that seemed to say *I will work you to the bone, but I'll take you to the top.*

The New Coach

Lasha quickly shut the door and hid behind it.

* * *

When she got home after the meeting, Lasha went straight to her bedroom. She turned to her corkboard, which was covered in red ribbons from the races she'd won over the years. Usually the sight was a source of pride. But on her first day on the job, Alexia had dismissed Lasha's past victories as being "mediocre."

Lasha needed to see the corkboard empty. A board empty of awards would push her to work as hard at swimming as Alexia would command her to. Ribbon after ribbon, Lasha removed them all. Finally, she held the oldest, most tattered one in her hand. It brought her thoughts back to the day she won her first red ribbon.

Nine-year-old Lasha's stomach had been full of butterflies the day of her first swim meet. She couldn't wait to beat everyone in the pool. She had also been excited that her new best friend — her only friend at her new school — was coming to watch.

When the school bell rang, Lasha and her bubbly, red-headed pal Ginger had leapt out of their seats. They'd made a mad dash to the school parking lot, where Lasha's dad had been waiting. In the minivan, Lasha had taught Ginger team cheers and they'd giggled all the way to the pool.

Lasha and Ginger had held hands right up until

it was time for the first race. Ginger even stayed by Lasha's side while Coach George gave her the pre-race pep talk.

"Are you nervous?" the coach had asked kindly. Lasha had nodded, smiling broadly. *My first race! Watch me. I'm gonna WIN.*

"Okay Lasha. Remember, the most important thing is to have fun. But while you're at it, remember to kick really hard and count how many strokes you take going into the flip turn. You don't want to miss the wall. Now give me a high-five!" Lasha had smacked his hand and then Ginger's before running off to the starting blocks.

"Take your marks . . ." Lasha had crouched into position. Then, BANG! The starting gun sounded and Lasha took off. As soon as she hit the water, all her nervousness had vanished. Her big feet and knobby knees on land turned her into a swimming machine in the water. Even then she had had long arms and big hands with strong fingers that pulled her through the water with ease. She had gained more ground with each stroke. As soon it was over, one of the officials had handed her a red ribbon that said "First Place." Lasha had been almost sad that she'd won the race so easily.

That ribbon had been the first of many. Now thirteen, Lasha stood in her room, ribbon in hand, savouring the memory. She pinned the single ribbon back on the board and hid the rest away in a box. Looking at the almost naked corkboard, she imagined herself winning a big swim meet. She cranked the music on her hand-me-down CD player and slipped on her Yorktown racing suit. She stood in front of her full-length mirror. She was tall and lanky, and the awkwardness she had felt when she was nine was now gone. She waved to a pretend crowd as if she were marching along the deck to the starting blocks.

She said aloud, imitating a sportscaster's voice: "And in lane number four is three-time National Champion, two-time World Cup winner, Lasha Boyko." Then she waved again at the pretend crowd.

"Take your marks. Bang!"

Lasha pretended to swim. She lunged forward, touching the mirror as if it were the touchpad at the end of a race.

"The crowd is going wild here at the aquatic centre!"

Lost in her fantasy, Lasha raised her fist in victory. "Boyko has set a new national record in the two-hundred-metre breaststroke. That's her fourth consecutive national title."

Lasha gave a final wave to her imaginary fans, then she dropped to the ground and began to do push-ups. She did twenty push-ups at a time until she reached one hundred. Then she did four sets of fifty sit-ups. She was about to repeat the set when her bedroom door flung open.

Her older brother Pete stood in the doorway. He

looked down at Lasha, who was sweating and out of breath. "You're so weird," he said, shaking his head.

Lasha wiped the sweat off her forehead. She didn't bother explaining. She knew Pete didn't understand why she was working so hard. The way he saw it, Lasha was the favourite. She went to private school, and the whole family made sure she got to swim. All Pete had gotten was a beat-up old car this year when he'd turned sixteen. And he only got *that* so he could pick up Lasha from practice three nights a week after his part-time job at a garage.

"Mom and Dad said your new coach is a real piece of work."

"Yeah, she's pretty scary," admitted Lasha. "What else did they say?"

"They said they think this new coach can make you some kind of champion."

"Really? They said that?"

"Ha! Yeah, but I doubt they *really* believe it. I mean, do you really think *you* could be a champion?" he asked, the doubt clear in his voice. "That new coach has put stars in everyone's eyes."

Lasha didn't respond. *Dreaming had to start somewhere, right?*

"They also said they're worried your grades will drop. If you're too tired from training, you won't get your homework done. They think you might fail at school. Again," he added after a pause.

It stung Lasha to be reminded of her near failure in grade three. Lasha wished she had Pete's brain. He barely studied but got all A's.

"I won't," Lasha said, trying to sound confident. She had already given up any social life to swim. If she had to keep her grades up too, she didn't know what else she could sacrifice to squeeze it all in.

"You'd better hope you don't. Or it'll be bye-bye swimming." Pete gave her a smirk, turned on his heel, and left her alone to think.

2 THE BULLY AND THE BOY

"Lasha, the audition results are posted for the school play. *Please* come with me," pleaded Ginger.

Lasha didn't even have time to shut her locker before Ginger was pulling her toward the theatre doors. When they arrived at the casting list, Lasha watched as Ginger stood on tiptoe to look for her name at the top of the list. Only her name wasn't there.

"I'm *so* sorry Ginger," said Lasha. She knew Ginger loved acting and singing as much as she loved swimming. But, unlike Lasha, who had the build for her sport, Ginger was short and plump, and not exactly what most Hollywood actresses looked like.

"If they want to give the lead to Missy, it just shows what the drama teacher knows about talent. Nothing!"

"Missy's got nothing on you." *Except that she's tall and blond and popular,* Lasha thought. *It's so unfair.*

"Well then . . ." Ginger's brave act crumbled. "Why didn't I get the lead?"

"I don't know, Gins. Maybe her parents bought the part for her!"

That's the way things seemed to work at Birch Hill Junior Private School. If your grades were slipping, parents would make an appointment with the principal, chequebook in hand. A donation to the library or the phys-ed department went a long way toward getting A's.

"Hm . . . Do you think I should have asked my dad to buy ME the part?" asked Ginger, her lips starting to form into a small smile.

"You know your dad would never do that!" Lasha said, even though she knew her friend was half joking.

"I know. It SUCKS," said Ginger.

Ginger's family and the Boykos came from similar backgrounds — hard-working, honest, Eastern European immigrants. The difference was that Ginger's dad had come from Serbia with only twenty dollars in his pocket and had built an auto parts empire, while Lasha's parents still struggled.

Despite her family's money, Ginger wasn't like the other kids at Birch Hill. If she had been, the girls might never have stayed friends. Ginger had been a nerdy "brain" and Lasha was the new kid in search of a friend when they met. By the time they had giggled themselves silly over their grade four teacher, who let out the worst smelling farts, they were best friends for life.

"I dare you to ask your dad," taunted Lasha as they headed back to her locker.

"Yeah, right!" laughed Ginger.

Lasha put her arm around Ginger and gave her a hug.

"You know what? I may not be Cinderella in the play, but I'm going to be the best evil stepsister that ever played the role," said Ginger.

"That's the spirit. You'll show them they messed with the wrong redhead!"

"Now if the play had been *Annie*, I would have been a shoo-in!"

They both giggled as they reached Lasha's locker.

"Oooh, poor little Ginger doesn't get to star in the play?" cooed Amy from three lockers down. On cue, the group of girls hanging around Amy snickered. "And I guess that means Lasha won't get to tag along with the star of the show."

"What's that supposed to mean?" asked Ginger.

"You know . . . Lasha's always trying to hang out with the HAVEs even though she's a HAVE-not . . ."

No matter how many years passed or how good at swimming she was, Lasha would always be known as the poor kid among all the rich kids at Birch Hill.

"Shut up, Amy! Yeah, yeah, your daddy is rich. And guess what? You're a spoiled brat." Ginger was one of the few kids in the school whose family was richer than Amy's.

Lasha tried to look busy searching for something in her locker.

"What's the matter, Cabbage Roll, are you gonna cry?" Amy taunted.

Lasha cringed at the nickname. One day, Lasha's mom had packed Ukrainian cabbage rolls for her lunch and the smell of cabbage had filled the cafeteria. Even though Lasha felt like crying, she didn't. If she cried whenever Amy picked on her, she'd be a slobbery mess all the time.

To Lasha's relief, Amy's attention shifted to her boyfriend, John, who was coming down the hall. *All hail the prince and princess of the Birch Hill kingdom,* thought Lasha.

But to her surprise, John came to Lasha's defence. "Come on, Amy! When are you going to drop the Cabbage Roll nickname? How many times do I have to remind you that your grandmother is Polish?"

Amy shot him an icy glare.

"Shut up!" she spat.

"Come on, ladies," she commanded her friends. "Let's blow this Popsicle stand."

On her order, the three other girls turned and strutted down the hallway behind Amy like they were on a Paris runway.

Lasha quickly packed her book bag. Now it was Ginger's turn to comfort Lasha. "Come on, I'll walk you to your bike."

As they headed down the hall, Lasha felt like someone was watching her. Unable to resist the feeling, she took a quick glance back. John was looking at *her*. The school's star quarterback? What were the chances that he would not be put off by the fact that she wasn't wearing designer shoes?

Lasha smiled shyly at him, then put her head down and made a beeline for the exit. She'd never really thought that the prince might be different from his princess.

3 THE PUSH-UP TEST

Lasha locked up her bike on the rack beside the community centre. Once inside she breathed in the familiar air, heavy with the scent of chlorine. Usually one breath of the moist air put Lasha at ease. The pool was like her second home, but today it felt different.

The chance to train under a *real coach* — one with a proven track record for producing Olympians — was like a dream come true. Goosebumps formed on her arms when she thought about the future. *This practice is the start of a new beginning.*

She tiptoed across the change room, stepping only in dry spots as she made her way to her locker. She was fishing around the bottom of her swim bag for the new goggles she had bought to mark the occasion, when a teammate hollered in.

"Lasha!"

Startled, Lasha straightened quickly, banging her head on the locker door. "Ouch! WHAT?"

"Hurry up! Coach Alexia wants everyone out on

deck. Now!"

"I'm coming!" Lasha gathered her things and ran for the door to the pool deck. She stopped briefly in front of the mirror to check out the small red bump forming on her temple and flatten some wisps of her mousy brown hair.

She walked across the cool deck and took a deep breath to calm herself.

As she got closer to the meeting area, Lasha noticed an unusual quiet — there was no radio playing in the distance, no hum from the boiler room, and no chatter coming from the group of twenty swimmers standing around.

Worried that she might be late, Lasha squinted to see the clock on the far wall. It was only 3:45 p.m. Practice didn't officially start until four.

She blinked hard to see against the glare of the sun through the atrium windows. She could only make out the outline of Alexia. She seemed to be dressed in a track suit, and she was standing by the basket of flutter boards. Beside her was the man from the Parents Meeting. When Lasha joined the group, the man smiled at her. Alexia passed Lasha as if she were invisible.

"Okay, everybody, sit down," Alexia ordered. She and the man pulled up chairs while the swimmers settled on the floor.

Alexia's piercing black eyes swept over the swimmers. When it was Lasha's turn to be sized up, she sat up straighter and tried to look the coach in the eye. She knew she had a good body shape for swimming — long lean legs, narrow hips, and squared-off shoulders. But the intensity of Alexia's glare made Lasha look down at her toes.

With a grunt, the coach wrote a few notes on her yellow notepad.

The swimmers began to shift restlessly in the long silence that followed, but the coach seemed in no hurry to put them at ease.

Finally, she spoke. "Go around the circle. Stand up and tell me your name, specialty stroke, and best race times. You start," she ordered a boy named Kevin.

Alexia took notes as they each shouted out their stroke and times like soldiers to their drill sergeant.

When it was her turn, Lasha was anxious to boast her best times. She wanted to impress the coach. "Lasha Boyko. Breaststroke. But I also sprint freestyle. I *almost* qualified for Junior Nationals in the fifty-metre freestyle. Best time: 28.88."

"ALMOST? Almost counts for nothing!" spat the coach. She looked Lasha up and down again. "You'll never be a sprinter, that's for sure." Alexia laughed, but Lasha didn't see the humour. "Sprinters are bigger and stronger than you. You have a body for endurance. Breaststroke and distance freestyle is where we'll focus."

How dare she say I'll never be a sprinter, Lasha thought angrily. *She hasn't even seen me swim!* But Lasha kept quiet. She folded her long limbs back into a cross-legged, seated position.

"All right, listen to me very carefully. Nothing I've heard here is very impressive. It is going to be hard work — lots of hard work and commitment if you want to improve. If you want to stay in this swim club, you must give me one-hundred-and-ten percent all the time. No crybabies." The swimmers looked nervously at one another. Coach Alexia seemed pleased that they looked scared.

Except for Lasha. *I'll show her!* she fumed.

"Morning workouts will start at 5:30 a.m. every weekday. Afternoons, you be here ready to start at 4:00 p.m. If you do well, we'll finish before 7:00 p.m. Wednesday afternoons will be for recovery, so you go home and rest. Saturday mornings we train at 7:00 a.m. Sundays you sleep in one hour, we start at 8:00 a.m."

If the swimmers had looked scared before, now they looked terrified. Twenty-five hours of training per week was much more than they were used to.

"Excuse me, Ms. Alexia?" said Kevin.

"Call me Coach, and stand up when you talk to me."

Kevin stood up, grinning. "How many of those workouts are optional?"

Alexia stood up to face Kevin, nose to nose. He was six feet tall and skinny. She was six feet tall and muscular.

"Your only *option* is to quit the program and swim with the babies."

The smirk left Kevin's face.

"No babies!" repeated the coach.

Kevin bowed back into his sitting position at the coach's feet. Satisfied, Alexia returned to her chair.

"This is Marcus," Alexia said, finally introducing the man next to her. "He is the assistant coach. You will listen to him like you listen to me."

Marcus's smile broke some of the tension in the air. But Alexia was quick to snuff out the warmth.

"Marcus will tell you our expectations. Marcus, please read the list."

The rookie coach cleared his throat. "One. You must be out on deck ready to go at least fifteen minutes prior to the start of practice." He looked up from the paper and smiled. "That means if practice starts at 5:30 in the morning, you need to be changed and on deck stretching or helping put in the lane ropes by 5:15.

"Okay, next — lateness and absence won't be tolerated. That one is pretty self-explanatory."

Lasha decided she liked Marcus. He seemed kind and slightly timid, or maybe he was just as intimidated by Alexia as the rest of them.

"Three. You will discuss with Alexia an ideal training weight that you will achieve and maintain. You'll weigh in every Friday. You are also to follow a low-fat diet as outlined in the Rathwell diet book. Ask your parents to get you a copy.

"Four. Girls will cut their hair so it is no more than ten centimetres in length. Um . . . this is so you can swim without a bathing cap. It lets your system stay cooler during hard workouts."

Many of the girls looked at each other in horror. Lasha didn't care about her shoulder-length hair. She thought it looked crummy no matter what she did to it.

"Five. Ah, this one is for the girls too. You must stop shaving. This will create more drag in the water for training. You'll shave down for competitions only. You'll learn more about that later.

"Six. No high heels, girls." He chuckled. "You're all too young for high heels anyway. We don't want twisted ankles getting in the way of training.

"Next, everyone must wear two bathing suits for practices. That's another way to increase resistance during training.

"Eight. Everyone must drink a full bottle of water every workout. You're going to be sweating buckets so it's crucial that you're replacing your fluids.

"Nine. No one will be excused to go to the bathroom. It disrupts your training momentum.

"And lastly, number ten. Parents may no longer watch practices."

So far so good, thought Lasha. There was nothing she felt she couldn't handle, although her dad would be annoyed that he couldn't watch practices anymore.

The Push-up Test

"Okay," Alexia said, once again commanding the group's attention. "Now I hope you have all been practising your push-ups and sit-ups. Let's see who will pass the test. Fifty push-ups in one minute, and fifty sit-ups in one minute. Lasha, you go first. Come to the front."

Lasha was used to being the example for the team. But usually she'd do dry-land exercises wearing shorts and a T-shirt. Today she felt awkward and naked in nothing but her bathing suit. She assumed a proper push-up position. *I've been practising. I'm ready for this.*

"Okay. You have sixty seconds. Now start!" Alexia ordered, starting her stopwatch.

Lasha's long arms and slender wrists were stronger than they looked. She had done thirty-seven push-ups when, after only forty seconds, Alexia hollered for her to stop.

"What do you call that?" Alexia demanded.

Still on her hands and knees, Lasha looked up at the coach. "A push-up?" she offered.

"That's not a push-up. Touch the tip of your nose to the ground. Then it's a push-up," growled Alexia. She forced Lasha's face down toward the grimy mats. "Touch your nose to the ground every time! Now start again!"

Coach Alexia reset her timer and Lasha started again from the beginning. But this time her pace was much slower.

"STOP!" barked the coach. "Time's up! How many was that?"

"Twenty-six," Lasha said, feeling cheated.

"Twenty-six then," muttered Alexia as she noted the number on her chart. Then she called for the next person. Lasha watched her teammates all pass the test. But she noticed that they didn't touch their noses to the ground.

"Now, get into the pool and give me three-thousand metres as a warm-up," Alexia ordered. The coach made a few more notes on her clipboard as she observed her new team. Then, shaking her head, a scowl on her square face, she turned abruptly and walked away.

Technically, I didn't pass the push-up test, thought Lasha, as she watched the coach disappear into her office. *Does that mean I have to go to the lower level? Did I fail out of the senior group?*

Lasha felt sick to her stomach. She had felt this way once before — when she had almost failed in public school. That time, Lasha had been sitting quietly outside her classroom waiting for her mother. She'd known she wasn't in trouble. The meeting was because Miss LaFleur, Lasha's teacher, thought she was "behind." The Boyko family had moved to Yorktown mid-year. She was so behind the rest of her grade that the teacher sat her with the grade two kids in the split class.

After twenty minutes or so, the office door had opened. Mrs. Boyko had grabbed her daughter's arm and hastily pulled her down the deserted hallway. "Come sweetheart, let's go home," she'd said. Lasha could tell that her mom was angry.

Lasha's mom hadn't spoken again until they were in the car. "Miss LaFleur says you're having trouble in school. She thinks you might have to stay behind a year if you don't improve. She even suggested that you might do better in another school — Lawrence Hill, which is closer to our house. She's arranged for us to check it out — you know, to see if you like it."

Lasha had froze. She may have been new to the neighbourhood, but she knew that the "dumb kids" went to Lawrence Hill School. Everyone made fun of the Lawrence Hill kids.

Lasha had whimpered. "I'm not stupid!" she cried, tears beading in the corners of her eyes.

Lasha's mom had looked at her, shocked, and almost ran the car off the road. "Honey, no one said you are. Why would you say something like that?"

"Because kids who go to Lawrence Hill are called dumdums!"

"That's not true. They get extra attention, that's all — more help to learn math and reading. They have smaller classes. They're not dumb, they just need extra help."

Her mom's tone had done little to calm Lasha. She'd cried the rest of the way home.

Coach Alexia's voice snapped Lasha back to the swim practice. "Now that you're warmed up, I'll ease you into a real training regime. We'll start with eight times four-hundred metres — all freestyle, except four lengths of each one can be any stroke you want. Those four lengths have to be all-out effort. The rest should be medium effort with thirty seconds rest between them. As you swim, I'll be walking around to observe your technique."

Lasha spent the rest of the workout swimming her fastest to show Alexia that she was good enough to stay in her group. At the same time, she fretted, *This is easing us in? We're gonna be in trouble!*

★ ★ ★

After practice, Lasha locked her bike inside the change room so she'd have it to get to school the next morning. Then she headed outside to the parking lot, where Pete was waiting to give her a ride home.

"So, how was she?" asked Pete, as Lasha opened the car door.

"She was okay, I guess."

"You don't sound too excited. I mean, after all the hype." Pete took Lasha's tattered swim bag from her and threw it in the back seat. "Come on, baby!" he muttered, turning the key in the ignition. The car roared to life, and Pete revved the engine a few times to make sure it wouldn't give out. Then he threw it into drive and they peeled out of the parking lot.

"Well?"

"Well what?" asked Lasha, adjusting her seat belt. She didn't feel like talking about her awful first practice with Alexia, especially with Pete. Lasha liked having swimming conversations with her dad, not him. Pete never seemed to understand why she did what she did.

"What happened?"

"She's kind of mean," answered Lasha quietly.

"Mean? What did she do that was so mean?"

"She tested our strength with a push-up test. She stopped me after thirty-seven of them, because I wasn't doing them 'properly.' She made me start over and my arms were so tired I could only do twenty-six more. I ended up failing the test."

"You? Fail at swimming? Impossible. You're the wonder child of swimming!"

Lasha heard the sarcasm in his voice.

"I was the only person who had to do 'perfect' push-ups," she retorted. Then she decided not to bother arguing. "Oh, never mind!"

"What?" laughed Pete. "Geez, it's just swimming."

"You could be a little more supportive, you know!"

"Okay, whatever. Sorry."

The joke was over.

4 THE ZONE

A couple of months into the training schedule, Lasha was starting to feel truly beaten down. The workouts were harder than she'd ever imagined. Alexia was mean and difficult to please. Lasha hauled her aching body onto the pool deck for her eighteenth hour of training that week, only to hear Alexia's voice call her name.

"Lasha, I want to see you in my office."

Inside the tiny office, Alexia shoved a sheet of paper in front of Lasha. "I want you to look at these workout results. This is a swimming set performed by the current Junior National Champion in the two-hundred-metre breaststroke."

Intrigued, Lasha took the paper and studied the times, thinking, *Alexia has been giving me the same sets as a Junior National Champion!*

"You've already swum this set, but not as fast. You must start hitting the same times," Alexia said.

Lasha gasped.

"What? You think you can't do it?" barked Alexia.

Lasha was too scared to answer. She was thinking, *this is impossible.*

"Are you quitting before you even start?" growled the coach in disgust.

Lasha was still frozen.

"You know how to speak?"

"Yes," answered Lasha meekly.

"Then what is it you don't understand? You're a real mental midget!"

The insult stung more than Alexia would ever know.

★ ★ ★

After their talk with Lasha's teacher, she and her mom had gone to visit Lawrence Hill. Lasha was already calling it the "school for dummies."

"Guess what, honey?" her mom had said brightly. "The class will be going swimming today!"

Lasha could tell when she was being set-up — as if getting to go swimming would change her mind about the school.

When they got to the school, the principal escorted Lasha to the classroom and introduced her to a friendly looking young teacher. Lasha sat at an empty desk feeling a mixture of fear, nervousness, and anger. She patted her bag with her bathing suit in it for comfort.

Lasha looked around the room. The other students didn't look any different from her. But what really mattered was how everyone else saw them. The kids at other schools would laugh and call her slow.

At the pool, Lasha spoke to no one. She simply changed into her bathing suit and followed the instructor's orders. She wanted to dive right in and swim laps to show everyone what she was capable of. But the instructors only wanted the students to jump in, touch the bottom in the deep end, and come back to the surface. Half the kids couldn't even float. Lasha felt sick. She didn't belong there.

Lasha didn't even want to get in the pool anymore. She made up her mind that she'd run away from home if they made her go to this school.

When her mom had come to pick up her up after school, she'd asked, "So? Were the kids nice? Did you have fun swimming?"

"No," Lasha had answered. "The kids weren't nice. No one even talked to me, other than the teacher. And no, the swimming was not fun — it was awful. Most of them couldn't even swim in the deep end. They looked all spastic."

Lasha had paused, then said angrily, "I don't want to go to that school. I'm not like those kids. I'm not dumb and I don't need any 'special' help." Her voice was shaking. "I just need *regular* help. I don't want to go to school with the dumb kids who can't even swim. I won't do it. I won't go."

At the end of the year, Lasha and her mother had

met with Miss LaFleur again.

"Mrs. Boyko, there's no doubt Lasha is a bright kid. She's made some improvements, but she's still quite a bit behind and needs a lot more attention. Here in the public system, she's falling through the cracks. I don't want to see her fail a grade. That could have a lasting effect on her self-esteem as well as her ability to make friends," said Miss LaFleur.

"But going to Lawrence Hill, Lasha would get streamed into general level. She might never break out of it. What about a university education?" replied Lasha's mom, who had studied hard in night school to become a nurse.

"Can you hire a tutor for Lasha?" Miss LaFleur asked carefully.

"Yes, absolutely," answered Lasha's mom without hesitation. Lasha looked up to study her mother's face. She could see the lie there.

"If you hire a tutor for Lasha and she works through the summer to catch up on math and reading, I could pass her this year . . ."

Lasha felt like jumping up for joy.

" . . . but there's one more condition," added the teacher sternly.

Lasha held her breath.

"If she won't go to Lawrence Hill for extra atten-tion, you need send her to a private school. At a private school, classes will be smaller and the teachers can devote more time to Lasha. It'll be expensive, but I need to know that's the plan for her."

"Agreed," said Lasha's mom, nodding. "I don't care what it costs . . . education is too important." She shook Miss LaFleur's hand.

★ ★ ★

"Well Lasha, are you going to quit before you even try?" repeated Alexia.

"No," said Lasha. She decided right then and there that she would never show Coach Alexia doubt or surprise again.

"Good," spat Alexia as she kicked the desk drawer shut. "The Junior Champion can swim this fast in workouts because she breaks the pain barrier. That is what you need to do. Breaking the pain barrier takes guts and willpower. But once you break through it, you'll start training at levels equal to the top breaststrokers in the country — and eventually, the world. I'm not talking just junior swimmers either."

Lasha listened. It all seemed farfetched. She couldn't believe that if she worked harder the pain would stop. *I'm already working as hard as I can!*

"You'll have the chance to try breaking the pain barrier tonight. I'm going to have you swim this set, a T-30." Alexia held up the paper. "You swam it before, but tonight I want you to break through."

Lasha was already working harder for Alexia than she had ever worked before. And now she would have to swim for thirty minutes as fast as she could — the dreaded T-30. Under her old coach, she had pushed herself only just beyond the pace of a leisure swim for T-30s.

"When it really starts to hurt, don't give in to it," lectured Alexia, her voice getting louder. Lasha could hear the emotion in it. "When it feels like you're going to die, keep pushing harder and harder. You must learn to deal with the pain. You have to beat it, or you'll never be more than a good club swimmer."

Lasha bit her lip. She thought of her goals — she wanted to be better than a good club swimmer. Determination washed over her. *What I really want is to be a champion,* she thought.

Lasha puffed out her chest bravely. She would find out if she really could make the pain go away.

★ ★ ★

Lasha was well into the T-30. She could hear Coach Alexia yelling at her from the sidelines as though Lasha was the only swimmer in the pool. Every one-hundred metres, Lasha peeked at the time clock on the turn. To her surprise, she was holding pace with the times Alexia had shown her. With each lap that Lasha saw she was still on pace, she became more determined to *stay* on pace.

Lasha could feel the new strength in her from the

months of training under Alexia. She was tired, but at the same time she'd never felt stronger. Surprising herself, Lasha found the inner strength to push harder.

Bring it on! Bring it on!

But soon her temples began to pound. Her body temperature was rising fast. Lactic acid was building up in her muscles, making them burn.

She checked the clock — she was still on pace.

Go harder! she told herself.

Lasha's eyes started to roll back into her head and her ears began to ring. She could barely see or hear, or make out the time on the clock. Lasha became unaware of anyone or anything else. Pain was all there was now. It was almost unbearable. Lasha took stroke after stroke in agony.

Bring it on! Go harder! Break through!

The pain Lasha felt became so intense, her mind started to shut down. She felt as though her soul had left her body to get away from the awful sensations. And then, amazingly, the pain stopped. It was just as Alexia had described it. She had broken the pain barrier — she was in The Zone! She felt as though she was floating over her body, watching it swim without a mind to slow it down.

The bizarre feeling lasted for a good fifteen minutes. Suddenly, a distraction thrust her soul back into her body and all the pain returned like a high voltage jolt. Lasha's system crashed. She felt like she was having a seizure. But she kept stroking, trying to regain her motor control for what was left of the T-30.

All the sights and sounds of the pool returned. She could hear Alexia screaming from the sidelines, "Pick up the pace. Go, go, go!"

Lasha finished the T-30. She had never experienced anything so hard in her life. Her face felt flushed and, getting out of the pool, she grabbed her water bottle and emptied it over her head to cool down. She braced herself, afraid that Alexia would yell at her for falling out of The Zone at the end.

The coach approached with her usual stern expression. But what came out of her mouth shocked Lasha almost as much as her own performance in the pool had.

"Nice work, Boyko."

5 ART CLASS

"I'm off to drama class. We're working on the play."

Lasha and Ginger were gathering their books from their lockers before the bell rang to signal the start of the school day. Lasha's hair was still damp from morning practice and her muscles were tingling from the workout.

Coach Alexia's training regimen was getting harder by the day. A handful of swimmers had already dropped out. But after Lasha's performance the night before, there was no way that she was going to quit. When they'd reviewed her times after practice, Lasha had matched the time of the Junior National Champion until the last three hundred metres, when she'd crashed. But the biggest surprise had been what Coach Alexia had said next: "Keep training like that and you'll not only go to Junior Nationals, you'll win at them!"

Lasha shook her head to bring her back to the present. "How's Missy doing in the lead role?" she asked.

A big smile crept across Ginger's face. "Oh, not bad, except the teacher is constantly trying to keep her *in tune!*" The redhead laughed her bubbling laugh. "Not me though, I'm killin' it!"

"Are you thinking what I'm thinking?"

"Well, if you're thinking that I'm going to outshine her until I get the lead role, then yes, I am!"

"You go, girl!" Lasha and Ginger did their high-five, low-five, tickle-the-palm secret handshake and walked off to class grinning.

But Lasha's smile faded when she got to art. It was usually her favourite class, but today it stopped her dead in her tracks. The desks had been rearranged. Her heart skipped a beat when she saw that her workstation was now right next to John's. Lasha sucked in a deep breath and, playing it cool, said hello to the teenage heartthrob as she sat down.

"Hi," he replied. Lasha was surprised to hear how shy he sounded.

Lasha blushed and buried her head in her watercolour. *If you can break the pain barrier, you can break the shy barrier too,* she coached herself.

"Oops, I think I'm using way too much water. My paper is getting all wrecked."

John looked up from his painting.

"Yeah, that was happening to me too. Try dabbing it." With a nervous shrug, he showed her how he dabbed his brush on a paper towel.

"Playing football again this year?" Lasha knew full well that he was.

"Yeah . . . yup, I am." He looked up and their eyes met for a second.

"How's the season going?" Lasha said, trying hard to get a conversation going.

"Um, it's okay, I guess. We're second in the district so far." He tried to appear engrossed in his painting.

"What position do you play?"

John put down his brush and looked at her with a funny smile. "You don't know what position I play?"

"No, sorry. I don't really pay attention to what's going on around here." Well, that was mostly the truth. It was only John she had been checking up on.

"It's 'cause you're always swimming, right?" he said.

Lasha was pleased that he knew about her swimming. He seemed interested about her athletics, too.

"Yeah. I've pretty much got my head underwater for four hours a day. So, as you can imagine, I don't have a lot of extra time on my hands."

"Wow, four hours a day. I thought two hours of football three times a week was a lot!" John seemed surprised at just how serious an athlete Lasha was. "What time do you practise? I mean, to fit in four hours a day?"

"Well, morning practices run from 5:30 to 7:30 a.m. Then afternoon practices are from four till six, sometimes seven, except Wednesday night, which we have off."

"Wow, you must be really good." It sounded more like a question.

Lasha was proud that she had become a star on the team, out-training everyone. But she didn't want him to think she was bragging, so she avoided the answer. "You never told me what position you play."

"Oh, I'm the quarterback," he replied quickly. But then he turned the talk back to Lasha's swimming. "I've only just heard about people who train that much. So you must be really good?" he said again.

"Yeah sure, I guess . . . I still have a lot of room for improvement. My coach thinks I will qualify for the Junior National Championships next month. She thinks I have a shot at placing in the top five."

"In the whole country?"

For once, Lasha didn't hold back. "Yeah. Maybe I'll even win!" She broke into a grin.

"Wow, that's serious business."

"Yeah well, it definitely takes up all my time."

"You must really love it."

That made Lasha think. Before Coach Alexia, Lasha's answer would have been a resounding ABSOLUTELY! But Lasha had been so focused on her goals that she hadn't really thought about her feelings for swimming in a while. Coach Alexia had been knocking her down with her "reign of terror," as Lasha had come to call her bad temper. And Lasha was exhausted all the time.

"That's tough to answer," she said slowly. "Honestly,

I love the feeling of winning. And I like the support from my friends and family — that sort of thing. The training's not very fun, though. Diving into a cold pool every morning at 5:30 a.m. isn't glamorous! So I wouldn't say I love training, but I do love winning, and training is what you have to do to win."

"I *really* love football," John said dreamily. "I only wish I could be as good at it as you are at swimming."

"I'll have to check out a game," said Lasha.

"Yeah, come. Bring Ginger. You two would have fun."

"Okay."

"Maybe I could check out a swim meet one day too."

Lasha's eyes opened wide in surprise. "SURE!" she said, all lit up. Then, embarrassed, she quickly turned back to her painting.

6 THE QUALIFIER

"Lasha, you have to think of yourself as better than this regional meet. With the goals we have for you, it's not enough just to win this weekend. You have to win with a handicap," lectured Coach Alexia.

Lasha, dripping wet, shifted on the cold wooden bench at the side of the pool. The rest of the team was still in the water, swimming up and down the lanes. Lane one, right next to Coach Alexia, was kept free for Lasha, while other swimmers were doubled or tripled up in their lanes. They were having an easy workout so they wouldn't be too tired for the meet that started the next day. The weekend-long event was a last chance to qualify for the Junior National Championships.

It was also the first swim meet since Alexia started coaching her. Everyone who supported the swim club, from the parents to the board of directors, were eager to see how the swimmers would perform. Everyone wanted to know if Alexia was worth what they were paying her.

"To challenge you and your thinking, I'm going to have you swim a difficult set tonight instead of resting," continued Coach Alexia.

Lasha groaned inwardly. She had really been looking forward to joining the rest of the team in an easy night for a change.

"Then," continued Coach Alexia, "at the meet, you're going to compete in every single event instead of just your best events. So, not just the breaststrokes. Everything — the sprints, the distances, the butterfly, and even your worst events, like the backstroke races."

Lasha's eyes widened. She'd never heard such a crazy idea in her life. Lasha would get very little rest between events in the preliminaries. And if she made the finals, her races would be practically back-to-back, only minutes apart.

"And," Coach Alexia continued, "you're going to double up your training bathing suits instead of wearing a racing suit, so you'll be held back by drag. And I want you to WIN at the meet."

Lasha opened her mouth to protest. But no words came out. In the short time that Alexia had been her coach, she had already programmed Lasha not to question or doubt anything she said. Instead, Lasha silently nodded.

"Since you'll be swimming all the events at the meet, you might as well practise them all tonight. Dive in and start a set of twenty by two-hundred-metre individual medleys — that's two laps butterfly, two laps backstroke, two laps breaststroke and two laps freestyle. Swim the first one slow, the second one medium, the third one with eighty percent effort, and the fourth one from a dive in an all-out effort. I want one-hundred-and-ten percent! Cycle through that pattern four times. Take thirty seconds rest between them. I'll be timing you."

★ ★ ★

At the regional meet, the pool deck was packed with hundreds of swimmers. There were dozens of meets like this one going on all over the country, as hopeful swimmers raced to qualify for the Junior Nationals. The Yorktown team had been bused to the event and were spending the weekend in a cheap hotel.

Lasha sat with her teammates in their corner of the deck. Sometimes swimmers would have to wait an hour between events. They passed the time playing cards, reading novels, or playing video games with friends. But since Lasha was entered in every single event, she was up to swim every half-hour.

During one of her breaks, Lasha tiptoed around her teammates and made her way across the busy pool deck to where her Dad was acting as starter for the races.

"Swimmers, take your marks." Her dad's voice was amplified by a small speaker so the whole row of racers could hear. When all the swimmers were spring-loaded in their ready positions, he fired the electronic beep that signalled the start of the race.

The racers were off. No false start.

"Hey there! What's up, kiddo?" asked Lasha's dad, stepping down from the starter's podium.

"Just coming to say hi," she replied.

"So, correct me if I'm wrong here, but I'm pretty sure you've made it into five finals for tonight. Even the fifty-metre freestyle — you must be excited! I thought Coach Alexia said you'd never be a sprinter. Tonight is your chance to show her, eh?" He tousled Lasha's damp hair.

"Yeah, I'm not a bad sprinter, despite what Coach Alexia thinks."

"Hey, I have an idea. I'm going to be the starter tonight for the fifty-metre freestyle final. After I say, "take your mark," just get into your ready position and go. I'll hit the beeper on your move. You'll get a couple tenths of a second lead right off the start."

Lasha wasn't sure if her dad was joking. He had been an official at her swim meets for years. He had always been the first to nail her if she did anything illegal, like touching the wall with only one hand on a breaststroke turn, or grabbing the lane line to pull herself along in backstroke.

"Okay, let's do it," she replied, her tone half-joking. After all, she was swimming SO many events, what did it matter if she messed around with one little two-length race?

"Seriously though, let's talk breaststroke. What does Coach Alexia expect tonight in the finals?"

"She thinks I should win hands down . . . and drop my time a good twenty seconds. Coach Alexia doesn't think it's good enough that I just qualify for Juniors. I have to get in there ranked among the top contenders," answered Lasha. Her tone was as matter-of-fact, like Alexia's when she dictated demands to her.

Lasha was neither doubtful nor confident at the moment. She was simply curious to see if all the work would pay off, as everyone hoped it would. And she didn't know what to think about the "handicap" Alexia had set up for her.

"Well, no matter what happens, you're my girl! And I'm proud of you." Then he added, "But I know you'll do it," and gave her a bear hug.

★ ★ ★

"Y-O-R-K. York! Goooooo YORK! Go Lasha! Wooooo!"

Lasha could hear her teammates cheering her on from the side of the pool as she readied herself for the fifty-metre freestyle sprint. It was her fourth final that night. She was on a bit of a high. Everyone on deck had noticed that she was up to something special

— swimming every event and doing well at all of them.

Lasha still wasn't sure if her dad was serious or not about their jumping-the-start scheme. On the starting block, she made eye contact with him. She grinned, and he winked back at her.

Woohoo . . . he's going to do it!

"Take your mark," he announced.

Lasha crouched down and then fired herself off the blocks. Mid-air, she still hadn't heard the starter's signal. Then she heard the *beep, beep, beep, beep* that meant a false start.

What? Oh, man! I'm going to kill my dad! Lasha stopped dead in the water and popped her head up.

She was the only swimmer in the pool. She looked over at her dad and scowled. He was at the sidelines, laughing.

All eyes were on Lasha. Everyone watched as she swam back to the wall, climbed out, and reset herself on the block. *How embarrassing*, she thought. *Dad totally punk'd me!*

Lasha could hear the laughter in her dad's voice as he announced the start again.

Lasha stifled a smile. Her dad's little joke had cut through her nerves, and she realized that he had probably planned it that way.

The second start was good and Lasha shot off the blocks and swam her best time of the day.

But after the race, her relaxed mood didn't last.

"You have a short break here. Go in the warm-down pool and work some of that lactic acid out of your system with a few laps," ordered Coach Alexia.

Lasha trotted off to the side pool and flopped into the warm water.

Alexia hadn't given Lasha any instruction so far that night. The coach was just letting her race, race, and race again. But before Lasha's next final, her best event, Alexia visited her at the edge of the warm-down pool.

"Next up is the two-hundred-metre breaststroke. Of all these races, this is the one that really matters. Pour every ounce of energy you have into it. But don't spin your wheels. Make every stroke count," commanded Alexia. "You're up now. Let's go."

Up on the diving blocks, Lasha bent down into the starting position and noticed her legs were shaking with fatigue. She didn't have time to think about it, as the beeper went off and the race began.

The cool water enveloped her as she dove in, as smooth as a dolphin. A long pullout, and — pop — she came up and began stroking. In the water she felt stronger than she ever had. She remembered what Coach Alexia had said about winning hands down. With a surge of energy, Lasha quickly pulled ahead of the other swimmers.

After that T-30 performance, a quick two minute and forty second race is a walk in the park, she thought.

Securely in the lead, Lasha felt she could have

coasted and still won. But with every stroke, her head popped up to the sound of Alexia's bellowing voice driving her on. As fatigue set in, Alexia's voice grew stronger and more forceful. Lasha pushed on harder and harder until she broke the pain barrier. She entered The Zone — pain vanished and the muscles in her body took over. She was stroking long and hard and fast; keeping a firm grip on the water — never slipping or wasting precious energy.

At the final turn, Lasha touched with two perfectly level hands and whipped her long legs around to the wall. For a split second before her push-off, she glimpsed Alexia, deliberately positioned in Lasha's sight-line. The coach's face was angry. Coach Alexia pointed toward the finish line, giving Lasha the clear order to finish the race with all her might.

Alright Lasha, you can do this.

Well in the lead, with no competitor to push her, Lasha knew her race was a mental one. It was her will against her body's pain. As determined as ever, she dug deep and mustered every bit of strength she had. She shot off the wall for the final length.

C'mon, Lasha! It's do or die time.

Lasha bit her lip and held her breath for a long, deliberate pullout. As her body glided smoothly, she relaxed her muscles for a second of recovery before popping up for the final twenty or so strokes it would take to get to the finish line.

Yes, yes, go, go. You, can, do, this! Lasha told herself in tempo with the strokes. The end was in reach. Lasha gave one last, hard kick and buried her head to stream-line herself. She soared forward like an arrow to reach the wall and stop the clock.

Goggles off.

She'd won the race hands down, but the win wasn't what mattered. It was her time that mattered. How her time stacked up against the times of the many dozens of swimmers winning races like this all across the country was what was important now.

The pool didn't have electronic timers, so she had to wait for her race time. In the meantime, she looked up at her dad at the starter's podium. He was waving his stopwatch around, trying to tell her something, but she couldn't hear. He looked really happy, and Lasha took it as a good sign. Then she glanced over at Alexia. Although her coach looked stern, she gave Lasha a small nod.

Lasha climbed out of the water. The timer in her lane told her her time: 2:39:01.

YES! She'd not only made the Junior Nationals' qualifying time, she'd destroyed it. This swim would place her firmly in the top ten breaststrokers in the country.

Lasha's moment to savour the victory was short-lived. Coach Alexia's whistle sounded, signalling her to get her butt into the warm-down pool.

7 DETENTION

"Each lap around the school gets you one craft stick," hollered the Birch Hill gym teacher. "To pass the fitness test, you need to get six craft sticks in sixty minutes."

All the students were grouped in the parking lot, dressed in their gym uniforms. They were sectioned off into their usual cliques — Amy and her posse were off to the side, looking put out about having to be seen in gym clothes; John and his football teammates were joking around at the front of the line. Lasha and Ginger were huddled in the middle, waiting for the signal to go.

"If you don't make it, you have to do it again in one month. So give it everything you've got. We don't want to see any of you out here again in the freezing cold!"

Lasha shivered and adjusted her toque — it was the only thing keeping her damp head warm. She'd just swum an eight-thousand-metre workout and had barely had a chance to dry off.

"I hate Mr. Johnson's fitness testing," complained Ginger.

"I know," sympathized Lasha. They both knew that Lasha would breeze through the test with no problem. *But ask me to hold a note like Ginger?* Lasha thought. *Forget it.*

"Ready everyone? Go!"

The footballers and track team shot off. Lasha and Ginger started at a medium pace. Amy and her gang waddled along in the back of the pack.

"Lasha, you don't have to go slow just for me," said Ginger.

"You know, I'm a bit tired from this morning's practice. We did eight thousand metres and Coach Alexia was on another rampage. She's made it a theme week. Everything we're doing is in four-hundred-metre intervals. It's her idea of fun!"

"Sounds like a blast." Ginger was already beginning to breathe heavily.

"Oh, it gets better. She made us do the four-hundred-metre butterfly four times! My shoulders are killing me!"

"She's such a maniac!"

Lasha hung back with Ginger for two laps.

"Okay, John is about to lap us," said Ginger. "Lasha, you've let me hold you back for two laps. You run and keep up with him . . . show him what a jock you are!"

Lasha looked at Ginger with shock. She hadn't even told her best friend about her crush yet. *Is it that obvious?* she wondered.

"Okay," giggled Lasha.

Before John caught up with them, Lasha turned it on to make him chase her a bit.

Eventually he caught up. "Hey, you're hard to catch," he huffed. He turned on the speed to pass her.

Pretty soon Lasha was running up to lap Amy. She passed the blond without saying anything, but she noticed that Amy was running flat-footed and her breathing was all wrong. *It's no wonder she's struggling*, thought Lasha.

Eight minutes later, Lasha was about to lap Amy again. Amy was red in the face and clearly hurting. Lasha thought about helping her. But Amy would just be mean to her, as usual, so she let her suffer.

Eventually, Lasha was upon Amy for a third time. Amy was gripping her side and limping a bit. The good sportsman in Lasha got the best of her, compelling her to help a struggling athlete, no matter who it was.

"Amy, breathe in through your nose and out through your mouth. It'll help you."

"Get away from me, Cabbage Roll!" heaved Amy.

Lasha slowed down to a trot to stay next to her.

"No, I'm serious. You're making it harder for yourself. Do what I tell you and the pain will be less, I promise."

Amy glared at her, but she was listening.

"Breathe like you're breathing from the pit of your stomach, not your lungs. See, it's my stomach that moves when I breathe . . . not my chest. Try that."

Amy and Lasha slowed to a walk. Amy tried breathing deeply a few times.

"Okay, let's just walk until we get to the end of this field. Then we'll jog again."

John whizzed past them. He did a double-take when he saw Amy and Lasha together. "Go, Amy!" he called out. Then he shook his head in disbelief and kept running.

"Okay. Now you're going to start jogging again. Try not to be flat-footed," continued Lasha. "You have to roll your step. Land on your heel then roll forward to your toes and give a little push-off. Rolling like that will give you forward momentum, 'cause right now you're just going *thud thud thud.*"

Amy glared at her again.

"Heel-toe, heel-toe, heel-toe," instructed Lasha, watching Amy's running technique improve before her eyes. "Hey, you're getting it. Now don't forget to breathe from your stomach. In through your nose, out through your mouth."

Amy nodded and plodded on.

"I have two more laps to go. I'll check on you when I'm done." Lasha took off like a gazelle to finish the test.

Mr. Johnson handed her a last craft stick. "Nice job, Boyko. You're done."

"Thanks, Mr. Johnson. I'm going to catch up with

Amy and help her finish," she shouted back as she kept running. She could see Amy not too far up ahead.

"How's it going?" asked Lasha when she caught up with Amy.

"Go away!" spat Amy.

"You look a lot better, and you're almost done. You can make it if you keep it up," said Lasha, ignoring Amy's order and focusing on how she was running. "Come on, a little faster now . . . keep up with me. Don't let this stinky Cabbage Roll get ahead of you!" Lasha was amazed how good it felt to help Amy.

Amy took a deep breath — through her nose — and picked up the pace to keep in step with Lasha.

Lasha checked her watch and paced Amy for two more laps.

"Amy, you can do it! You're gonna make it! Go!" hollered Mr. Johnson as he handed off her fifth craft stick. "Don't let up! Lasha, pick up the pace a bit — she's got eight minutes left."

Lasha checked her watch and picked up the tempo.

"Alright Amy, you can do this. Just think — if you don't go for it now, you'll have to do it all over again next month."

Amy looked at Lasha, a terrified look in her eyes.

"Okay. Let's go," Amy puffed bravely.

John rallied the football team to cheer for her. Pretty soon everyone was chanting, "Amy, Amy, Amy!"

Lasha could see that it was helping. She checked her

watch — time was tight, so she sped Amy up a bit more. Amy crossed the finish line with twenty-five seconds to spare.

Everyone cheered.

"Nice job, Amy!" said Lasha.

"Thanks," said Amy, before flopping into John's arms.

"Thanks, Lasha. She would never have finished if you didn't help her," John said to Lasha.

"No problem. I didn't mind the extra laps," she blushed.

★ ★ ★

"Hurry Lasha, we're late for class!" Lasha and Ginger were sprinting up to the third flight of stairs to the science wing. Lasha stopped to catch her breath on the second landing. She was exhausted from her swimming workout and then the run.

Lasha looked up at the last set of stairs and felt defeated. "Ginger, you go," she called out breathlessly. "I need to stop."

Lasha plopped down on the step and rested her head on her knees.

"I thought you were some kind of athlete," joked Ginger as she backtracked to where Lasha was sitting.

"I'm spent. I can't. I'll be there soon." Lasha was sweating from the exertion. "I just need to rest for a second."

"You've got to be kidding. You're telling me that you can't make it up these stairs, but you'll be able to go to practice this afternoon and swim, like, ten kilometres? Give me a break. Get up!" ordered Ginger with a laugh.

They reached the science lab a few minutes late, but the teacher let it slide. Lasha headed for her seat in the back. As she passed Amy's desk, Amy turned her head as if to look out the window. John, seated next to Amy, lowered his eyes, embarrassed by the obvious dis. But Lasha was almost too tired to care.

Twenty minutes into Mr. Dean's biology lesson, Lasha's eyelids started to get heavy. She shook her head and slapped her cheeks gently to wake herself up. It was a losing battle. The teacher's voice became a lullaby and she drifted off to sleep. The last thing Lasha heard was Amy snickering at her and John snapping at Amy to be quiet.

Lasha didn't know how much time had passed before — WHAM! — Mr. Dean's biology textbook slammed down on the desk next to her head, waking her with a start.

Frightened, groggy, and totally embarrassed, Lasha looked around. Everyone was laughing, except Ginger and John, who were both cringing.

"Miss Boyko, science class is not nap time. Now tell me, what is the role of mitochondria?"

"Um . . . sorry. The answer is . . . um . . ."

"Never mind, young lady. Go to the principal's

office and explain to him why you think it's okay to take a nap in my classroom."

"Yes, sir."

Lasha slowly rose. Her limbs were numb and tingling. Upright, she stood nose to nose with Mr. Dean, who shrank back slightly.

"I'll take notes for you, Lash," offered Ginger.

"Maybe those extra laps were too much for you, Cabbage Roll," spat Amy. Her friends all snickered.

Lasha saw John elbow Amy and give her an icy glare.

"What? Why are you always sticking up for her anyway?" Amy growled at him. She gave him a shove.

"Amy, she saved your butt this morning. If it weren't for Lasha, you'd be out running laps in the snow next month," scolded John as Lasha left the classroom.

Lasha rubbed the sleep out of her eyes and bravely headed for the principal's office.

★ ★ ★

"The principal will see you right away," said the secretary, smiling sweetly. Lasha liked the secretary — ever since she and her parents had first come to the school to discuss ways to pay Lasha's tuition, the secretary had seemed kinder to her than to the other students.

But the principal wasn't as friendly. And Lasha knew why. Mr. Rexhamer had to be serious because he was directly accountable to the rich and powerful parents who funded the private school.

"Lasha Boyko. Falling asleep in class. Unacceptable. Why did that happen?" he asked.

"Well, I'm really tired lately from training. We have a new coach and she's making us swim twice a day — morning and night. And the workouts are really hard. The fitness test this morning must have put me over the edge. I was just plain tired, I guess."

"Mr. Johnson told me what you did for Amy this morning. That was very sportsmanlike of you."

"Thanks," Lasha said, using the back of her hand to cover a yawn.

"I didn't know you were such an athlete. And running isn't even your sport — you're a swimmer. Give me a report." Mr. Rexhamer was all business, but Lasha knew he liked it when his students were special.

"Since the new coach started, my best time has dropped about twenty seconds. I've already made the Junior National Championships," bragged Lasha. She repeated what she had told John. "My coach thinks I could be in the top five in the country at the Championships."

Mr. Rexhamer straightened his tie and looked thoughtful. Then he changed the subject abruptly. "What can you do to guarantee me that napping in the classroom won't happen again?"

"Drink tea after lunch?" offered Lasha. She wasn't trying to be smart, just knowing that her options were limited by Coach Alexia's training schedule.

"Drink tea. That's your solution?"

"Yes. I think that might help. I just need a little caffeine boost to get me through the afternoon."

"How are your grades? You came to us because you were having trouble in the public school system, if I remember correctly."

Lasha's heart jumped. "My grades are pretty good now, sir," she responded timidly.

"It's a financial strain for your parents to send you to this school, isn't it?" he asked.

"Yes," murmured Lasha, looking down at her hands in her lap.

"So, is it fair to say that you should be trying your very best in school to justify the sacrifices your parents make for you?"

"Yes."

"So I ask you again, how can you guarantee you will never fall asleep in class again? And please give me a better answer than a caffeine fix."

"Um . . . maybe go to bed earlier and make more effort to pay attention in class? Also, I could ask Mr. Dean to move me closer to the front." She hoped those were the answers the principal was looking for.

"That's better. Now, report to detention after school today."

"Oh, I can't! My swimming coach will freak."

"Well Miss Boyko, you should have thought of that

before you fell asleep. That's the problem with youth today; you don't consider the consequences of your actions. Detention from 3:30 to 4:30 p.m. Dismissed."

Oh there'll be consequences, thought Lasha as she left the office. *Coach Alexia will kill me!*

★ ★ ★

Lasha spent the whole time in detention stressing about how Alexia would react to her arriving at practice almost an hour late. Nobody had ever been late before, so there was no way to guess what Alexia would do.

When the clock hit 4:30, Lasha jumped out of her seat and bolted for the door. She gathered her books from her locker in record time and ran for her bike. She almost barrelled over John and Amy as she rushed out into the early winter cold.

"Hey, slow down there," yelled John good-naturedly. But Lasha hardly saw him; she *had* to get to practice.

Lasha banged her old bike around trying to unlock it from the fence. Frantic, she quickly pulled it to the sidewalk and jumped on. But her first push was too forceful, and the chain popped off the gears.

"No, no, no . . . please no!" she cried, panic rising in her.

Lasha tried to put the chain back on, but it wasn't cooperating. Soon her fingers were black with grease.

She heard John and Amy approach before she saw

them. "Hmph, look at her. Grease monkey!" Amy said.

I wish my brother was here. He could fix this easy, thought Lasha, not wanting to look up.

"Amy, why are you always so mean to Lasha?" she heard John say.

"Why do you defend her?"

"I'll do more than defend her," John said. "I'll help her, just like she helped *you.*"

Lasha glanced up in disbelief from where she was kneeling beside her bike. She saw Amy huff and march off.

John was walking over to her. "Hey, Lasha, need some help?"

My hero, she thought, as John started fiddling with the chain.

"My coach is going to have my head on a platter if I don't get to the pool ASAP," she said.

"Well, you're out of luck with this chain. The metal is twisted here, so even if we got it back on, it would pop right off again."

"Oh God. It's going to take me twenty minutes to get up the ridge on foot. The bus takes too long to come." Lasha was close to panicking.

"I'll double you on my bike." John offered, unlocking a sturdy mountain bike.

Lasha blushed, but this was no time to be shy.

"Okay. Thanks."

"You sit on the seat and I'll ride standing up," he said.

They hopped on and she inched her arms around his waist nervously.

"Hang on tight!" he hollered back at her as his legs got to work.

"Woohoo!" shrieked Lasha as they bumped over a curb, making John laugh.

Lasha smiled all the way to the pool.

8 THE QUITTER

The whole swim team was well into their main set for the evening workout when Lasha came running onto the pool deck, huffing and puffing. Coach Alexia stayed on the far side of the pool and ignored her. It was Marcus who called Lasha over.

"Hey Lash, what happened to you?" His friendly manner was hardly a comfort to Lasha when she knew Coach Alexia would lecture her before practice was through.

"I got a detention in school for falling asleep in biology class. I was so tired, y'know?"

"I gotcha! Well, the team is a quarter of the way through their main set. Why don't you jump in lane six and do a fifteen-hundred-metre warm-up. Mix it up a bit."

"Is Coach Alexia mad?"

"Oh, you know Alexia. Of course she's mad. But hey, don't sweat it. She only picks on the good ones, right?"

Lasha dove in and started her warm-up, keeping a watchful eye on Coach Alexia. Before long, Marcus headed over to talk to the coach. Lasha could tell from Alexia's body language that she was *gonna get it.*

Alexia spent the rest of the workout paying attention to the other swimmers. There were only twelve left of the twenty who started on the team. Usually Marcus took care of them while Coach Alexia hammered on Lasha. The break from being the team "star" was relaxing, but it made Lasha realize how left out the other swimmers must feel most of the time.

Lasha planned a quick getaway for the end of practice, hoping Coach Alexia wouldn't catch hold of her. But the second Lasha pulled herself out of the water, her coach was right there, waiting.

"Come with me." Alexia's black eyes looked scarier than ever. Lasha took a deep breath and followed the coach into her office.

"I don't want to hear your excuse. I don't want to hear any crap! I don't care why you were late. No matter what the reason . . . it's your fault. You control what happens in your life. The fact is that you missed almost an hour of training."

"I'll make it up if you want."

"Make it up? You mental midget! Workouts are laid out with a certain amount of time off in between to recover. They're designed to build on what you've achieved the day before. If you miss a workout, that practice is gone. You can't make it up."

"Sorry," whispered Lasha, still dripping wet.

"Sorry means nothing. Tomorrow morning, you come in one hour earlier. This is not a makeup work-out. Be ready to swim at 4:30 a.m. instead of 5:30. Now, go home. You've wasted enough of my time."

Lasha hung her head and left the office. She wasn't as upset about being punished as she was knowing that she had screwed up.

★ ★ ★

At 3:45 a.m. the next day, Lasha tiptoed into her parents' bedroom to wake up her dad. Normally she rode with a car pool, but only her dad was willing to drive her at this hour.

"Dad," she whispered, hoping to stir the snoring giant without waking her mom.

"Dad, time to wake up . . . Dad." Lasha glanced at the clock nervously. She didn't want to risk being even ten seconds late for practice. If she was late, she knew that Coach Alexia would blame her for not waking up her dad earlier.

She shook her dad harder. "DAD!"

"What! Who! Where!" Her dad jolted awake and sprang out of bed, fists raised.

"Dad, Dad, it's okay. It's just me, Lasha. No one's here but me."

"Oh, sorry." He rubbed his eyes and leaned over to peer at the clock on the bedside table. "How long before we have to leave?"

"Fifteen minutes."

"Okay, sweetie . . . I'm up."

Lasha's dad had found the whole "punishment" sort of amusing. His daughter never got detentions or got in trouble for anything. He had seemed relieved that Lasha wasn't just a swimming and studying robot.

A few minutes later he came into the kitchen, teeth brushed, face washed, sweatshirt and jeans on. "Go scrape the frost off the windows and start my van. Let it warm up for five minutes," he ordered Lasha gently. "It dropped below freezing last night."

"There's not enough time to let the van warm up!" Lasha hadn't budgeted time for that.

"Sorry, honey, that old beast won't run if she ain't warmed up."

"Dad, I can't be late. I'm already in trouble for being late yesterday!"

"Well, darling daughter, you'd better get out there and start scraping."

Lasha flew outside and started scraping the frost off at record speed. Then she ran inside and hauled her dad out.

As they drove off into the pitch-black early winter morning, Lasha was grateful for the peanut butter and jam sandwich and bottle of orange juice her dad had handed her. She watched the clock and shifted anxiously every time they hit a red light. At 4:15 they pulled into the parking lot. Lasha kissed her dad on the cheek, then dashed inside.

Coach Alexia was already pacing the pool deck. She looked like she'd been up for hours. Her hair was perfectly slicked back, her shorts and golf shirt neatly pressed.

With less than a minute to spare, Lasha appeared on the pool deck, her hair still lumped to one side from sleep.

There were no "good mornings" between Lasha and her coach. "Take lane one and warm up with one thousand metres of freestyle. I want you to get fired up. This morning's practice is going to be very demanding and I want to see one-hundred-and-ten percent effort from you. You have tonight off, so leave all your energy in the pool. After warm-up, you are going to swim five-thousand-metres breaststroke. I want each thousand metres to be faster than the previous one. There will be no stopping for rest."

That's the craziest thing I've ever heard! It's the same length as the annual Swim-A-Thon distance. And she wants me to swim it by myself — and all breaststroke! Lasha was freaking out, but outwardly she didn't flinch. She wouldn't give Coach Alexia the satisfaction of seeing her rattled.

Coach Alexia clapped her hands together, the signal

to get moving. Lasha put on her cap and goggles. She kept repeating in her head, *don't think about it, just do it.*

After her warm-up, Coach Alexia readied her stopwatch. The first thousand metres were easy and took Lasha twenty minutes.

"Good! Now go a little faster!" Coach Alexia's instructions were barely audible to Lasha, but she got the gist of it.

Lasha could see her pace time on the giant digital clock at the side of the pool. Lasha did the math in her head: if she was to get faster every thousand metres by, say, ten seconds, she'd be swimming at an impossible pace by the end.

Then it dawned on her: *Oh no, I started too fast!*

Another thousand metres down. Alexia gave Lasha the signal that she was still on pace, but the waving for her to go faster became more forceful. Lasha's knees were beginning to ache.

At the three-thousand-metre mark, Coach Alexia stopped her. "Boyko, you're not focusing! Make sure you are streamlining every stroke! Where is your head?" yelled Alexia.

Not only was this set painful, it was boring. Lasha started a wordplay game to keep her mind occupied. One word per stroke. One letter per one hundred metres. It helped her keep count of the laps.

Apple, attic, attack, attach, arrange, appearance . . .

Turn. Push off.

Book, boot, bum, battle, beetle, beach . . .

The rest of the team began to file in at 5:30 a.m. Marcus tried to usher them into their lanes for their own workout, but they were all fixated on what Lasha was doing, curious to see what her punishment was.

"Faster! Faster! Faster!" screamed Coach Alexia, red-faced, from the sidelines.

By four thousand metres, Lasha's muscles were fatigued and she was losing motor control. She forced herself to concentrate on keeping her strokes long and strong.

One more kilometre to go. That's still forty laps! I can't keep this up!

Coach Alexia stopped Lasha briefly.

"Is that it? Is that all you've got! Girl, if you're only going to give it half an effort, you won't amount to anything! If that's all you've got, you might as well hit the showers. I don't want to watch any more crap. Now pick it up — this is the last thousand. Give me everything you've got!"

The breathless athlete furrowed her brow and pushed off the wall, newly motivated by anger. Despite the pain in her knees, her shaky muscles, and her burning lungs, she pushed harder, trying to achieve The Zone.

Lasha hurt so badly she was fighting tears, but Coach Alexia's intensity only increased. With sixteen lengths to go, Marcus rallied the rest of the team to cheer Lasha on to the finish. Her teammates whistled, whooped, and banged their flutter boards on the side of the pool, making a thundering noise that gave Lasha goosebumps and the strength to finish.

Five kilometres of breaststroke DONE!

Exhausted, she hauled herself out of the pool. Her teammates patted her on the back, clearly relieved not to have been in her shoes. "Way to go. Lasha, you're the MAN!"

All Lasha could think was, *thank god it's over.*

Coach Alexia quickly shooed them all away. Lasha briefly wondered if she'd get a pat on the back from the coach, too.

But instead, Coach Alexia leaned in and said, "I want twelve fifty-metre sprints from a dive. I want them FAST."

"What?" asked Lasha, crushed.

"You heard me. Get up on the blocks."

Lasha didn't move. Her knees were swollen from hours of repetitive movement, her head pounded, and she felt nauseous.

"NOW!" Coach Alexia barked.

Lasha prided herself on her "bring it on" attitude. But this was too much. Tears welled up in her eyes as she crawled up to the starting block and tumbled back into the water.

"Pick it up!" shouted Coach Alexia between whistles and hollers as she followed along the pool's edge.

"What the hell do you call that? That was ludicrous!"

she yelled when Lasha finished the first sprint. "Get up again and make this one less than forty seconds! If you don't get the times down, you're going to keep repeating them until you do!"

I can't. It's too much. I can't.

Lasha lumbered through the water, choking back sobs. She tried to block out her negative thoughts with visions of winning the Junior Nationals.

If I can do all of this, then a measly two-hundred-metre race will be a cakewalk.

But her times got slower and slower every sprint.

Alexia launched into a tirade after the eighth one. "You gave up! Are you a quitter? Are you going to quit like this in a race, Lasha?"

All Lasha could do was hold her stomach and listen.

"If I were you I wouldn't even show up to practices. What's the point? Is that all you want, to be just another mediocre swimmer? I've seen about as much crap as I can take for one day, Lasha!" Alexia stormed off toward her office.

Lasha stayed in place, staring down the length of the pool. There were still four sprints to go, but she didn't finish them. Conflicted and exhausted, she tried a couple laps to warm down, then crawled out and dizzily got ready for school.

For the first time, the thought ran through Lasha's mind: *Maybe she's right, maybe I should just quit.*

★ ★ ★

An hour later, Lasha stumbled into class, feeling like she'd been hit by a ton of bricks. Her clothes were a mess and her pale face still showed splotches of red from the exertion.

Ginger came running over. "Lasha, are you all right? Why do you look so blotchy?"

Ginger grabbed Lasha by the hand. "You're all clammy. What has Coach Alexia done to you?" she demanded.

"I'm . . . Me? I'm a-okay," replied Lasha, feeling strangely giddy.

Alarmed, Ginger led her to the nearest desk.

"Brrr. Don't they have any heat on in this place?" Lasha rubbed her arms.

"It's hot in here, Lasha. You're sick. I'm taking you to the nurse's office."

Lasha's fingers were turning numb and her whole body was tingling. She tried to focus on Ginger's face but all she saw were dancing green dots.

"Ginger, I don't feel so great. I want to lie down. Where can I lie down, Ginger?" said Lasha getting up out of her seat. She instantly dropped back into it, afraid she was going to faint.

The rest of the class started to notice.

"Ms. Stevenson, Lasha is sick. I think she's going to pass out. She needs the nurse," said Ginger.

The teacher looked horrified at the idea of a student fainting in her class. "Yes, yes . . . take her to the nurse. John, help Ginger in case Lasha faints. What's wrong with her, anyway?"

"She'll be okay. She just needs to lie down," replied Ginger. There was no time to explain that Lasha had a psychotic Russian throwback coach who beat her to a pulp twice a day, every day.

John hoisted Lasha up. Even in the state she was in, Lasha admired how strong he was from playing football. *He's almost perfect*, she thought. *His only flaw is that he is dating Amy.*

Ginger followed them down the hall but took charge in the nurse's office. She explained about Lasha's new coach and the intense training to the school nurse.

"Can I help?" John asked.

"No, no. I've got everything under control now. I'm just going to give her some juice and let her sleep," said the nurse. "You two can both go back to class. You've been a big help."

Before Lasha drifted off, she heard the nurse on the phone to her mom. "Mrs. Boyko, this is the nurse at Birch Hill. It seems your daughter overdid it at her swimming practice this morning. She's been quite faint and delirious, but she's sleeping now. Perhaps you should pick her up and take her home to bed."

"No, I'm okay . . ." Lasha called out, not wanting her mom to have to miss work.

"Go to sleep, sweetheart," said the nurse, patting Lasha on the head.

Lasha did.

★ ★ ★

Lasha didn't know how long she slept before Pete woke her up.

"Hey, sis. Wake up," said Pete, placing his hand on Lasha's forehead. "Your chauffeur is here. Mom couldn't leave work so she had me pulled out of school to come and get you. She wants me to take you home and put you to bed. Nice to be you, eh?"

Then he turned to the nurse. "Is she okay? I've seen her tired, but never like this before."

"Apparently her training was a bit much this morning," replied the nurse. "But I think she'll be fine with some rest."

Lasha was so happy to see her brother that she felt like crying.

Pete pulled her to her feet and held her steady as they walked out to the parking lot. As soon as she was in the car, Lasha drifted off to sleep again, her head gently rolling from side to side.

In her dream, Lasha saw herself opening the freezer to prepare an ice pack. She iced one knee. *Now ice the other knee.* She wanted to move the ice bag, but she felt too paralyzed with sleep.

"Hey, Lasha. Hellooo? Wake up. We're home," said Pete.

"I need to ice my other knee," she muttered, feeling around her knee for the bag.

"What ice? There's no ice in the car."

"Yes . . ."

"No, Lasha. C'mon, get out of the car. I'll get you ice inside."

She looked at him with glazed eyes.

Pete gently guided his sister inside and to the sofa.

Through a haze, Lasha heard the doorbell ring. Pete went to get the door, and Lasha was surprised to hear Marcus's voice.

"Hi. You must be Lasha's brother, Pete," he said. "I'm Marcus, the assistant swim coach. Your mother called Alexia and told her that Lasha was dizzy and fainted at school. She said you were bringing her home, so Alexia asked me to check in on her."

"Yeah, I've seen you when I've picked up Lasha at practice. Come in."

Pete led Marcus to his sister.

Marcus quickly monitored Lasha's heart rate and breathing.

"Hi Marcus," Lasha said, patting Marcus on the hand as he took her pulse.

"What is Alexia doing to her?" asked Pete, still not understanding why his sister was barely conscious.

"Alexia is pushing Lasha harder than any other

swimmer in the club. I don't know if you know, but your little sister is an amazing athlete. Unlike most, she has the mental strength to push herself past normal body limits. This morning, Alexia really challenged her and your sister blew the coach's mind. Alexia set her up to do a set that only a few athletes in the world have ever done and Lasha performed pace times that were on par with the best ever recorded."

"They were?" Lasha muttered.

"Yes, Lasha, you did an unreal performance this morning."

"But Alexia was so mean. She called me a quitter."

"Sweetie, I don't know why she does that. Maybe it's because she wants you to keep fighting. Maybe she worries that if you think you're good, you might not try so hard."

"What do you mean, as fast as ever recorded?" asked Pete.

"Pete, Lasha trains as fast as the top swimmers her age in the world. If she can translate that into a race situation, there'll be no stopping her. She could go all the way. Alexia has all the proof she needs from this morning's swim to believe that Lasha can do it."

"Do what?"

"Do what? Make the Olympics one day, Pete."

"Wow! Geez, I had no idea," Pete said, sounding guilty. "I guess you're not just a weirdo, sis," he added, tweaking Lasha's nose.

Lasha patted him on the hand and floated happily into sleep, knowing that her brother didn't think she was a weirdo anymore.

All too soon, though, she heard Coach Alexia hollering, "What are you lazy no-goods waiting for? Get in the pool NOW!"

Quickly, the scared band of teenaged swimmers dove into the pool's freezing cold water. The sudden shock gave Lasha goosebumps. Through the gruelling workout, she watched the beastly trainer storm around the deck, brow furrowed, barking at the swimmers. When the coach came Lasha's way, Lasha cranked up her energy level and focused on perfect technique, but nothing she did seemed fast enough or good enough.

"What kind of crap swimming is that?" spat Coach Alexia in her thick Russian accent. "As soon as the going gets tough you fall off pace and your technique goes to hell. What's the matter with you? Don't you have the mental capacity to control your body? Or maybe you're just a quitter. Is that what you are, a quitter? Disgusting! Go hit the showers and don't come back!"

Lasha headed for the shower. A teammate was already rinsing shampoo from her hair. The sight triggered a strange feeling of déjà vu in Lasha, and she suddenly felt anxious. "Will you pinch me?" she asked.

"Why?"

"I've been having the same dream. They're more

like nightmares, really. I fall asleep and next thing I know, I'm in the middle of a really hard practice. It's all so vivid. I get sore muscles, Alexia yells at me, and I even get water up my nose. Only when I'm totally exhausted and burnt out does my alarm go off. The really awful part is that once I wake up, I have to go straight to the pool and endure the real thing."

"Really? That's awful!"

"Tell me about it. Anyway, I just got the feeling that the two of us standing here in the shower is just the end of another one of those dreams. I want to know that those eight thousand metres we just swam were for real. Because if this is a dream, I think I'll have a nervous breakdown!"

"You're seriously losing it," said the swimmer with a chuckle. She reached over and pinched Lasha's arm as hard as she could.

"Ouch!" yelped Lasha, sitting straight up. She was panic stricken and confused. *What time is it? Why is there daylight out? Did I sleep through my alarm? Did I miss practice?*

Slowly the events of the day came back to her. It was 4:30 in the afternoon, not the morning. She sank back into the couch and pulled the blanket around her, happy that she didn't have to get up and go to practice.

★ ★ ★

The next morning, Lasha's alarm chimed at 4:30 as usual. She felt refreshed, but her muscles were sore and she was hungry. She tiptoed quietly down the stairs to the kitchen and poured herself some orange juice. Within a few minutes, Lasha's mom came down in her robe.

She sat across from Lasha at the kitchen table. "I just hope this pays off for you, honey."

Lasha didn't reply.

Her mom sighed. "I'm making you some eggs."

"Ugh! No, Mom! Not before my workout. Gross! I'll burp eggs," she explained, feeling a twinge of guilt. After all, her mom just wanted to help.

"Are you sure you're okay?" her mom asked.

"Yeah, I told you, I'm fine," reassured Lasha. "Can I have some cereal?"

"Why don't you take it easy at practice today?" she said, as she poured Lasha a bowl of her favourite cereal. "If you're tired, just tell Alexia you have to go to the bathroom. Then go and lie down in the change room. How can a ten minute break make any difference either way?"

"Okay, Mom," replied Lasha, not mentioning Alexia's no-bathroom-break rule.

9 THE SCHOLARSHIP

The Boyko family was madly tidying up the house after dinner. Mr. Rexhamer had called and was going to stop by the house that evening to "talk about something."

"Well, did it sound like it was a good something or a bad something?" Lasha's dad asked Pete, who had taken the call. He bent down to scoop up some socks off the living room floor.

"I don't know. It sounded neutral. Stop grilling me. He said he wanted to pop by and was that okay? I said you guys were home and that was it," answered Pete. "Mom, where do you want this?" he asked, holding up a dustpan.

"Lasha, did something happen at school that you're not telling us? Do you think it has to do with detention and then missing a day of school? Did you miss a test?" demanded her mom, worry making her voice rise.

"I don't know. I don't think so. You guys are getting me all flustered!"

Lasha wasn't sure if her mom was anxious because

of what Mr. Rexhamer might have to say or because she only had twenty minutes to clean the house and make tea.

Ding dong. Everyone froze.

Lasha's mom and dad held hands and opened the door.

Mr. Rexhamer stood on the step. His winter jacket was unzipped and his tie was loosened. He smiled warmly at them.

As soon as they were all seated, Mr. Rexhamer got down to business. "Thank you for seeing me at such short notice. First, I want to assure you that nothing is wrong."

There was a collective sigh of relief around the room.

"Now, I don't want to take up a lot of your time so I'll just tell you the reason why I'm here. When Lasha had her little visit to my office, I had the opportunity to find out a bit more about her swimming. I didn't know until then that her swim club had hired a new coach and that the club was getting serious about being competitive. When Lasha told me that she'd qualified for the Junior National Championships, I thought right away that we might be able to support her in her athletics. Her achievement might warrant some kind of school scholarship. So I did a little investigating. I spoke to the school's board of directors and to Coach Alexia."

He turned to speak directly to Lasha. "Now, young

lady, if you can come in the top five at the Junior Nationals next month, the board of directors is prepared to give you a full athletic scholarship."

"What does that mean, exactly?" asked Lasha's mom hopefully.

"Mrs. Boyko, it means money — money toward tuition. It's enough to cover the rest of the year's tuition fees and all of next year's fees."

Lasha's mom gasped. Her dad's eyes widened and Pete looked like he had been socked in the stomach.

Lasha bit her lip. "What if I don't make the top five?" she asked. What they were talking about wasn't a sure thing — far from it. She'd never even been to a Junior Nationals before, let alone in the running for the podium.

"Well, Lasha, the board made it challenging because they only give athletic scholarships to students who truly deserve them. I'm sure you'll rise to the occasion. Your coach seems to believe in you, so now you have to believe in yourself and make it happen."

"Mr. Rexhamer, thank you so much for your part in this. Birch Hill has been so good for Lasha. I mean, who knows what would have happened to her in the public system. She might have fallen through the cracks." Lasha's mom was almost in tears.

"Yeah, Mr. Rexhamer, thanks," added Pete unexpectedly. Lasha realized that the scholarship would not only help relieve her parents' financial burden, but would also free up some cash for Pete. He had sacrificed too, just like the rest of the family.

"Well then, we'll all be watching with bated breath to see how our little rising star does at the Junior Nationals!" Mr. Rexhamer stood up to leave.

Lasha went to bed that night filled with a mix of excitement and fear.

★ ★ ★

Ginger was fully supportive of Lasha's crush on John. They went together to watch him play a round of tennis at lunch. It was one of the few days left before the court would be out of service for the winter. The outdoor courts weren't where Lasha and Ginger usually hung out — they were reserved for the in-crowd. Ginger walked carefully up the steep bleacher steps, holding down her miniskirt, while Lasha easily bounded up with her long legs in baggy jeans.

The only empty area on the crowded bleachers was near Amy and her followers.

"Come on, baby! This set is yours!" Amy shouted to John. "John is so much better than Jordan, I don't know why the score is even close. John must be having a bad day." Her voice was loud, to make sure everyone sitting nearby would have no doubt about who John was dating. Then Amy spotted Ginger. "Oh no, here comes Drizella!"

Ginger grinned triumphantly. "Actually, Amy, there's an opening for the Drizella part. I think you'd be perfect! Oh, except that you have no talent."

"Amy, didn't you know that Ginger outshined the leading lady? Missy stepped aside so Ginger could take the lead," announced Lasha proudly.

Amy turned and whispered something to her pack. They must have confirmed the rumour because Amy didn't look their way for the rest of the match.

Lasha elbowed Ginger and gave her a nod of approval. They settled in to watch the game. *"Woohoo!"* hollered Lasha when John scored a point.

John glanced up into the bleachers and smiled at Lasha.

It was Ginger's turn to elbow Lasha and give her a nod of approval.

★ ★ ★

"OMG! Lasha!" screamed Ginger on the other end of the phone line.

"What?"

"It's John! He just texted me that he wants your phone number. He wants to wish you good luck before Juniors."

"He did?" gasped Lasha, feeling her heart flutter. "Is he online right now? Message him back with it."

"Messaging your number right now."

Lasha could hear Ginger tapping speedily at her cell phone.

"Sent!"

They held their breath.

"Cool . . . he said cool. Maybe he'll call you. Let's hang up so he can get through. CALL ME AFTER!" ordered Ginger.

Almost instantly Lasha's phone rang. It was Birch Hill history-in-the-making . . . the hot quarterback calling the poor girl from the other side of the tracks. Lasha could hardly believe it.

"Hey Lasha, it's John." He sounded confident.

"HI!" she said too loudly, not doing a very good job of hiding how excited she was.

"Ginger gave me your number. Hope you don't mind."

"No, of course not. How's it going?

"Okay I think. Um, I broke up with Amy," he blurted out.

"Oh . . ."

"I feel pretty good about it. Like I feel relieved or something. She could be so mean, you know? Well, you of all people know, right?" He was rambling. "Anyway, she's pretty pissed off right now."

"Oh . . ." Lasha didn't know what to say. She didn't want to sound too happy.

"Well I think we're on different planets sometimes. She's so into clothes and appearance that I don't think I know what's real with her . . . if anything."

"Right."

"Plus she totally doesn't get sports. She doesn't understand what you did for her the other day. When she said thank you to you after the fitness test, I honestly think she was saying thank you for you telling her *good job*, not thanking you for helping her."

"Oh . . . I wasn't sure. I guess I figured that out later when she was as mean as usual," replied Lasha.

"Anyway, that's not why I'm calling. I wanted to find out when the Junior Nationals are and if I could come and watch," John said. He sounded happy to change the subject.

"I'd love that. They're in two weeks, but they're really far away. I'm flying there," said Lasha. *Why couldn't they be happening around the corner so John could come — so her whole family could come?*

"Oh, too bad," he said. He sounded disappointed.

"Well, maybe I could come to your football game," she suggested. "I heard there's one this weekend. I'd like to see YOU in action!"

"Hey, yeah! Absolutely!"

As soon as the call ended, Lasha dialed Ginger's number, giddy with happiness.

★ ★ ★

Saturday morning after swim practice, Lasha and Ginger

sat around Lasha's kitchen table making signs and banners for John's football game. They didn't care that they were being jump-on-the-bandwagon fans. They had reason to be.

"Amy must be so furious!" squealed Ginger.

"Honestly, I don't know what I did to make him want to call me," said Lasha. "But, hey, I'm not gonna argue! He's so cute and way nicer than I ever gave him credit for."

"He was always nice, for someone who grew up in Birch Hill. Nothing like Amy, who just got meaner and meaner as she got prettier and prettier. Good riddance."

"Can you believe this is the first football game we've ever been to? Where have we been?" asked Lasha, as she carefully dabbed sparkles on her bristol board. "All I know is that I want to show my support of him and his football — from one athlete to another."

Ginger held up her sign, which read, "Birch Hill Rovers Rule!"

"How's this?" she asked, proud of her colourful work of art.

"Yeah! Rovers Rule!"

Both girls laughed.

Only a handful of spectators braved the cold weather to watch the football game. Ginger and Lasha were huddled together, sipping from a thermos of hot chocolate, when the football team came parading onto the field like a band of gladiators. The girls jumped to their feet to hoot, holler, and hold up their homemade signs. John, who led the team, waved up at them with a great big smile on his face.

John huddled the team up and the game began. Lasha didn't really understand what was going on, but she was happy that the Birch Hill Rovers clobbered the other team by fourteen points.

After the game, John came to visit them in the bleachers.

"I loved watching you play today," said Lasha, trying not to gush. "You're such a strong player, a real leader. I can tell."

"Nah, I'm not that great. Not like you're great at swimming, I mean."

"Oh, stop it. I'll get a big head!" Lasha blushed.

"Lasha, you deserve to have a big head," laughed Ginger happily.

"So, what do your teammates think of the 'Cabbage Roll' cheering them on?" asked Lasha, a bit guardedly.

"Ah, I don't care what they think," he replied.

His answer made Lasha shrink into her seat. Judging by his tone, his friends obviously *did* disapprove of her.

"Well, I don't care what my friends think about me cheering you on either," said Lasha, trying to make light of the moment.

"Really? What did they say about me?"

Lasha was surprised at the hint of hurt in his voice. Despite all his good looks and money, was he insecure like everyone else?

"Oh, they say stuff like . . . why on earth would you want to watch some guy in tight pants hike a ball around?" replied Lasha with a smile. "Right, Ginger?"

The tension vanished and they all laughed.

When Ginger excused herself to go find a bathroom, John and Lasha huddled close together on the cold bleachers for warmth.

"You know, ever since your fainting incident, I've been watching you. You're nothing like the girls I've known."

"No?"

"No, not at all. They're all concerned about their hair and their clothes."

"Yikes, that makes it sound like I have really bad hair and bad clothes!" joked Lasha.

"No, no, no. That's not what I meant at all. No. Shoot. What I mean is . . ."

"It's okay, John, I'm actually kind of proud of my messy hair."

"Your hair is great and your clothes and everything . . . it's just that's *all* they care about — their looks, and sitting around gossiping. It's more like bad-mouthing people. But you're not into that. It's like you don't care about any of that. I really respect that about you."

"Thanks John, that means a lot to me."

He put his arm around Lasha and gave her a nice squeeze.

10 THE PRELIMINARIES

"Hurry Lasha, Marcus just pulled in the driveway!" Lasha's mom hollered up the stairs.

"Wheeee . . . okay, I'm coming!" screamed Lasha from her bedroom, where Ginger was sitting on her overstuffed suitcase. The two friends were struggling to force the zipper closed.

"I know I'm forgetting something. I just know it!" bubbled Lasha. She felt strong and healthy. She had survived Coach Alexia. Now she was ready for some serious performing.

"As long as you've got your bathing suit, your goggles, and your competitive spirit, that's all you need," shouted her dad from the hall. Lasha had been the only swimmer from the Yorktown Swim Club to qualify for the Juniors and her dad had been beaming with pride ever since.

"Coming!" Lasha picked up the pace when she heard the doorbell ring. "Thank goodness Marcus is coming on this trip too," she said.

"I know. I'd feel so sorry for you if you were going

with just Alexia. What a nightmare that would be."
Lasha knew that Ginger felt as if she too had been
tortured by the woman's maniacal training regimen.

"Now, I want you to call me after your swim," said
Ginger. "You promise?"

"I promise. If I had a cell phone, I'd call you from
the gold medal podium. Imagine, me on a podium!
The girl from Yorktown who's never even been on a
plane before!" dreamed Lasha.

"I can imagine it," broke in Lasha's dad. "You're
gonna get there, I know it. But first you've got to get to
the meet! Get your butt downstairs and into Marcus's
car before you miss your flight!"

Lasha's parents and Ginger gave her a big hug before Marcus whisked her way. Next stop was to pick
up Coach Alexia and then they were off to the airport.

Two days later, the competition was about to begin. On
the morning of her big race, Lasha wandered around
the Olympic-sized pool deck, wide-eyed. She had never
swum in such a huge pool. The Olympium had stadium
seating for two thousand, a diving well with a ten-metre
tower, an eight-lane, fifty-metre competition pool, and
another fifty-metre pool with six lanes for warming up
and warming down. Swimmers in a rainbow of team
uniforms were milling about, stretching, talking, and

laughing. Others were off in corners, mentally preparing themselves to race.

Hundreds of parents and fans were in the bleachers, waiting for the warm-ups to end and the preliminary heats to begin. Lasha felt a twinge of sadness that her parents weren't among them. Her dad had never missed one of her swim meets, but he couldn't afford to fly there and stay in a hotel.

Before the preliminary heat of the two-hundred-metre breaststroke, Alexia sat Lasha down. "Okay, Lasha. Now listen carefully. This is exactly how I want you to swim this race. Listening?"

"I'm all ears," replied Lasha, still peering around her unfamiliar environment. *Just being here with the top swimmers in the country, and being counted as one of them is enough,* she thought.

"Now you must be serious. This is no time for daydreaming. We didn't come all the way out here to lose."

Lasha tried to focus.

"Now, in the preliminaries, you must go all-out. You must beat all these other swimmers to be in the final tonight. You must not flinch. You must break through the pain barrier. Understand?"

"Yes," said Lasha, sneaking a peek at another swimmer passing by.

"Are you even listening?" barked Alexia. "This is how I want you to swim the race. Follow my instructions exactly."

Lasha's eyes started to wander again. Coach Alexia grabbed the girl's face and forcefully brought it back level with her own. "I know this is all very exciting and different for you, but if you screw this up because you're not concentrating, you won't be very happy. I won't be happy. I'm sure your parents, who paid good money for you to fly here, won't be happy. And they won't be too happy if you don't get that scholarship. So get your head screwed on, right now!"

"Sorry, sorry . . . I'm listening."

Coach Alexia furrowed her brow. "You are in a good lane at the centre of the pool, which means you have the fastest qualifying time of all the girls in your preliminary heat. You must beat everyone in your heat. If you don't, you will have almost no chance at making the finals. So, I want you to go out very fast. Be first off the starting block and be first at the end of the first length. Let everyone try to catch you for the rest of the race. You have the ability and endurance to hold the lead."

"First at the fifty-metre mark. I gotcha."

"You need to come in at 2:36:00 to be in the running. That will be a best time for you, but I think that's a time you're ready to hit."

Lasha nodded.

"Have you got it?"

"Yes. Yes. I can do that. No problem." Lasha was rocking back and forth.

"LASHA! Your head is not screwed on! You need to

focus. Seriously! I want you to find an empty hallway and regain your focus. I want you to get fired up. I want you to get so fired up that you feel like punching a wall. You have to be like a bullet ready to fire. Bang your head against a wall if that's what it takes for you to focus!"

Coach Alexia smacked Lasha's head.

"Ouch!"

"Get that head screwed on right, pronto!"

★ ★ ★

Lasha had a good half-hour before her race. She looked around the building for a quiet spot to try to focus. She settled down and took deep breaths. She tried to visualize herself straight through the race to the finish line and see herself winning.

Punch a wall to get fired up?

Lasha stood up and said out loud, "Win."

"Win!"

"Win!"

Each time she made a punching motion. Then she bravely punched the wall.

"Ouch!"

Lasha looked at her knuckles. Her hand was starting to swell.

What a dumb idea!

Lasha's throbbing knuckles distracted her a bit on the starting block, but she managed a fast dive. As she dove into the frigid water, she forgot all about the coach's instructions. At the fifty-metre mark Lasha was third and she had to play catch up the rest of the race.

The race seemed over too fast. Lasha was just finding her groove in the last length. She felt like she could have gained ground on the leader if the race had just had one additional lap.

Barely out of breath, Lasha looked up at the scoreboard to see her second place finish and her time of 2:37:35. It was a second and a half slower than what Coach Alexia wanted. Lasha's stomach turned. *Fun and games are over. Coach Alexia's gonna kill me.*

Lasha's race time was her personal best, but she knew she could have gone a lot faster. Now she was worried she might not make it into the finals at all. It all depended on how fast the swimmers were in the remaining three heats.

She walked over to the warm-down pool and waited for her trainer to tear a strip off her. But Coach Alexia was nowhere in sight.

Lasha swam a few warm-down laps, letting it sink in that she'd come all this way and screwed up big time.

Twenty minutes went by and still no sign of Coach Alexia.

Eventually, Lasha got so nervous she went seeking out her coach for the inevitable fallout. Lasha peeked around corners to try to spot Coach Alexia without being seen. She wanted to read the coach's body language to get a sense of what might be coming. Lasha stopped in her tracks when she saw Coach Alexia and hid behind a pillar to spy. Alexia looked strangely pleasant, smiling while talking with some other coaches.

Hmm, maybe she's not mad at me. Lasha left her hiding place and approached. After getting in a friendly last word with the other coaches, Coach Alexia turned to Lasha with a stone cold expression. She reached out and clamped a strong hand on Lasha's bony shoulder, steering her away from the crowd. To Lasha it felt like a death grip.

Coach Alexia cursed. She was standing so close that her coffee breath was hitting Lasha in the face. "Lasha, you really screwed that one up. You feel good now, you stupid little girl?"

Lasha cringed and lowered her eyes.

"What was the last thing I told you? What was the thing I told you to do in that race? What was the one thing?" Coach Alexia demanded, so furious she was practically frothing at the mouth.

"To be in first at the fifty-metre mark," replied Lasha timidly, still avoiding eye contact.

"That was the worst effort I've ever seen! You started that race way too slow! What place were you at the end of the first lap? Hmm? Did you even look? Or did you completely ignore my instructions?"

"I was tied with the pack of front-runners . . ." Lasha began sheepishly.

"Yes, you were all in a pack. But the time clock put you third at the first turn! Third! Now, are you trying to tell me that you were TOO TIRED in the first length to go any faster than that? Or do you not care enough to do what it takes to win in this sport? Or are you just a mental midget?"

Lasha could handle Alexia's screaming, but she hated when she called her a "mental midget." It brought Lasha right back to her troubled school days. Comments about her intellect shook Lasha's self-confidence more deeply than Coach Alexia could possibly have known.

Lasha raised her eyes to Coach Alexia, pretending that her pride was not shaken. The coach stared back at her, waiting for an answer.

After what seemed like forever, Coach Alexia gave up waiting for an answer and launched into a monologue. "You just about threw away six months of training. Let me tell you something, young lady . . . there's only one breaststroker in this whole country who you're not ready to beat the pants off. That's right. You've been training at levels higher than just about all of your competition, yet you let some bunch of no-name swimmers with not even a fraction of your talent or training almost knock you out of the finals. At this level, when it comes to racing, it's ten percent physical and ninety percent mental. This morning, you failed mentally."

"Did you say almost?"

"Almost what?" snapped Alexia.

"You said almost knocked me out of the finals."

"Yes, you snuck into the final in last place. That means you're going to be swimming in the far left lane. Are you proud?" Coach Alexia spoke as if the far left lane was the most shameful place on earth.

"Well, it was my best time and I made the finals at my first Juniors . . ." said Lasha, but she stopped when she saw Coach Alexia's face turn crimson and her nostrils flare. Lasha braced herself.

"You mental midget! You *would* think that," the coach spat. "After all the time I've spent training you and talking to you and trying to teach you what you're capable of, you say, 'but that was a best time, Alexia.' You know and I know that swimming a best time wasn't going to be good enough today. Today, you needed to have your head screwed on right and be looking at the bigger picture. But you're too dense to see it or believe it — I don't know which. All I know is that, because you didn't believe in yourself, you're now going to be swimming in an outside lane. It's the worst possible place to be."

Lasha tried to ignore the words being fired at her and focused on watching Coach Alexia's moving lips. They were cracked and she had a hairline scar over the left side of her upper lip. As Lasha studied the contours, she felt an overwhelming desire to reach out and clamp the flapping lips shut.

"I swear sometimes you look like you're not even listening, like you're off in some other world. You have a real focus problem and it's gonna cost you big time if you don't straighten out your head! You're always just nodding and agreeing, but I never know if you're hearing me. Are you really listening? Am I just wasting my breath?"

"No, no, I'm listening," Lasha replied. Shame burned through her veins.

"It's like I'm talking to a brick wall!"

Lasha rubbed her bruised knuckles.

Coach Alexia stomped around in a small circle, cursing in Russian.

"Listen, you're in eighth tonight. It's not where you belong but it'll have to do. Do NOT lose sight of your goal! I don't want another pathetic repeat of this morning. You know you're not the only one with a stake in how fast you swim!"

With that Coach Alexia stormed off, leaving Lasha with what seemed like the weight of the world on her shoulders. Everything was at stake — Alexia's coaching job, Lasha's parents' financial situation, and the club's image. Lasha squeezed her head hard between her hands.

Out of the corner of her eye she could see Coach Alexia and Marcus talking. Then Marcus made eye contact with Lasha and came over to where she was sitting.

"Hey Lash." Marcus's voice was cautious.

"Hi Marcus," she answered, on the verge of crying.

"So, are you excited? You get a second swim at your first ever Juniors!"

Lasha hid her bruised hand under a towel and heaved a sigh. "I guess so. At least it's a chance to do better than this morning."

"Now, don't let Alexia get you down. You've trained really hard to get here. You made the club proud even by qualifying to come here. And you've beaten, what . . ." Marcus opened his brochure to see how many breaststrokers were entered in the two-hundred-metre breaststroke event, " . . . forty or so top swimmers at one of the most competitive meets in the country to be eighth. It's fantastic!"

You set lower standards than Coach Alexia, she thought. Out loud she said, "I guess so."

Marcus's pep talk wasn't working, so he tried a different tactic. "I know how hard Alexia is on you. But she's only like that because it's so obvious that you've got what it takes. She's just excited and anxious to have you totally realize your potential."

They were silent for a moment. Lasha's mood felt about as low as the bottom of the deep end of the pool.

"I've got to tell you, Lasha," Marcus finally said, "Alexia knows everything there is to know about swimming. It's her life. For her, there's nothing else. This single-minded drive makes her bent on excellence. Your failure is like a personal failure for her."

"Oh thanks, Marcus, you're really helping." Lasha rolled her eyes.

"Let me finish," he said putting his arm around her shoulders. "Alexia's thirst for excellence is kind of obsessive."

Lasha nodded and looked up at him with puppy-dog eyes.

Marcus continued. "She is so blinded by her obsession for excellence that she forgets that we are all just humans. She forgets that we all make mistakes and have good and bad days and good swims and bad swims."

Lasha sighed.

"Alexia wants you to be happy."

"Come on!" Lasha said. *How could Marcus say something so ridiculous?*

"Well, see, that's the thing. Alexia actually does want you to be happy, and for her, happiness comes from winning. So she just wants you to do your ultimate best."

"Marcus, Coach Alexia doesn't care about my happiness. She cares about winning, YES, but happiness, NO. And taking care of my happiness is not her job; making me a fast swimmer is. If I expected her to make me a happy swimmer, I would have gone crazy a long time ago."

"Okay, you're right. So the trick to thriving under Alexia is to listen to what she says and not how she's saying it."

"You mean I should ignore it when she calls me stupid or quitter or idiot? Or her favourite, *mental midget*?" Lasha raised an eyebrow at Marcus, testing to see if he knew what sorts of insults the coach flung at her.

"Mental midget?"

"Yup."

"That's not right."

"No, I agree."

"You're sure a strong kid, Lasha. And don't worry about anything else. I'll take care of it."

"Thanks," replied Lasha. She was starting to feel a tiny bit better. She suddenly didn't feel so alone. At least now someone else knew about the way Coach Alexia talked to her.

"Well, anyway, just try to let all that stuff roll off your back," said Marcus. "Of course you're no mental midget! Just listen to the useful stuff and file all the rest of her ranting under G for garbage. She's set in her ways and I doubt she'll change her style now. Just trust me when I tell you that she really does care about you. As a matter of fact, she sent me over here to make sure you're okay."

"Really?" Lasha's eyes welled up with tears.

"Yes, sweetie, she did."

Lasha couldn't find it in herself to forgive Alexia. She didn't think anything could erase the negativity she had been enduring under the coach's reign. But that bit of information at least helped Lasha see Coach Alexia as a little human after all.

Lasha knew it wasn't the time or place to brood, so she changed the subject. "I'm hungry! Let's go get something to eat."

Marcus smiled.

11 THE FINALS

A few hours before warm-ups for the finals, there was a soft knock at Lasha's hotel room door. Not expecting anyone, Lasha peered curiously through the peephole. It was Coach Alexia. Lasha's heart skipped a beat. *What now?*

Flustered, Lasha opened the door and smiled nervously.

"Are you . . . um . . . how are you?" Coach Alexia asked awkwardly.

Such a common question sounded odd coming from Coach Alexia. Lasha realized it was because it was the first time the coach had ever asked it. "Fine," she answered.

This time it was Coach Alexia who was looking down at the ground. "I came down on you this morning because I want you to be as fast as I know you can be," she said softly. "Sometimes I forget that you're still young. I want you to know that no matter what I say, I only want what is best for you. I want to see you achieve your goals."

The moment felt so awkward that it left Lasha speechless. The words sounded familiar. *Marcus must have reported back to her,* thought Lasha.

"Okay, so, I am sorry for being so hard on you this morning. Tonight you concentrate like a good girl and you'll do great. I know it."

Lasha thought she saw a tear in the coach's eye. But before she could say anything, the coach stepped forward and briskly hugged Lasha. Then she turned on her heel and started down the hall. Lasha was dumbfounded. *Did Coach Alexia just apologize? Did she just admit she was wrong?*

When the door swung shut, Lasha broke down and cried for the first time since Coach Alexia entered her life. The coach's rants and the insults had never reduced her to tears, but her apology did. With every sob, it seemed that more pressure lifted from Lasha's shoulders.

★ ★ ★

Marcus drove Lasha to the pool for warm-ups. Coach Alexia seemed to be back to her regular, guarded self. Once again she sat Lasha down to talk to her before the race. This time, Lasha knew what to listen to — the words, not the personal attacks. But to her surprise, the coach took a new approach.

"Lasha, since I've been coaching in Yorktown,

you've been working really, really hard. You are probably one of the hardest working, most disciplined kids I've ever coached. You've stood up to every challenge I've placed in front of you and often exceeded my expectations. That T-30 test set and the five-thousand-metre breaststroke were milestones in your training. The times you posted have been some of the fastest anywhere in the world. I should have told you that then, because I've come to learn that you function best when you're happy. Some swimmers excel out of fear or need for approval, but that's not how you operate. Really Lasha, you should be happy with yourself. There is only a small handful of swimmers in the whole world that could do better."

Lasha's mind was racing. She had no reason to doubt what Coach Alexia was saying. She just couldn't believe she was hearing compliments and positivity from her coach.

"But training is not competition. So you need to translate all of that hard work into fast racing. You need to feel confidence in yourself, that you belong in the top rankings. All I can tell you is that everything I've seen you do in practice points to success. I want you to wrap your head around winning tonight. You're one of the fastest swimmers here. Trust me, I know. I'm paid to know such things."

Lasha nodded. *I can do this. I know it.*

"Lasha, you have the endurance, the discipline, and

the technique to beat every swimmer in that final to-night if you set your mind to it. Remember, you have out-performed every single person in this pool in training."

"Okay," said Lasha quietly. She could believe this. She had to.

"Because you're in the end lane for the final tonight, you won't be able to see your real competition — the girls in the fast middle lanes. So unlike this morning, I don't want you to worry about where anyone else is in the pool. Swim your own race tonight. Focus on start-ing off long and strong, then pick up the tempo every length. Leave no energy untapped, but stay in control of your strokes. Don't start spinning out of control. It's a waste of energy and gets you nowhere."

"Okay." Lasha knew she could do everything Alexia was asking of her. *After all, if I can swim five thousand metres breaststroke in practice, what was a measly two hundred metres?*

"If you just do all that, you'll do fine. Got it?"

"Got it," said Lasha smiling again.

Lasha had a look of sheer concentration on her face as she crossed the pool deck toward the Ready Room, where the finalists gathered before the race.

"Lasha!" called a familiar voice.

Lasha scanned the stands. Her eyes landed on a mass of red curls bouncing down the gallery steps. There was no mistaking it — Ginger was here!

Behind Lasha's best friend were her parents and Pete. Lasha couldn't believe her eyes.

"WE'RE HERE!" they all yelled. "SURPRISE!"

"Sorry we missed this morning, but we knew you'd make it into the final!" explained her dad.

"We drove!" exclaimed Ginger.

"Mom and Ginger are staying in the hotel. Dad and I have some sleeping bags for Hotel Minivan," said Pete, grinning.

Lasha just kept repeating *I can't believe it* and *thank you* as she hugged and kissed them all, eyes full of tears.

"Hey, you'd better go. They're calling your event." Her dad gave her back a pat, gently pushing her on her way.

Lasha walked away full of confidence — and overflowing with happiness.

★ ★ ★

It was standing-room-only at the Olympium that night. Two thousand fans had come out to watch their favourite swimmers compete. The marshals called the two-hundred-metre breaststroke finalists to the starting blocks.

Eight finalists, including Lasha, stepped into the spotlight. Music was blaring over the loudspeakers. Fans stomped their feet and cheered. Swimmers were banging kick boards against the bleachers and chanting, causing a deafening roar.

Lasha's heart was pounding. She'd never witnessed such a commotion for a swimming race before. She tried to calm herself, but she was shaking violently — not with fear, but with excitement.

The announcer introduced each of the eight finalists. As her name was announced, Lasha gave her family and Ginger a quick wave.

"GOOOOO LASHA!" cheered her brother above all the noise. Lasha smiled.

The starter blew his whistle and the finalists mounted the starting blocks. An unnerving hush replaced the noise of the crowd. Lasha crouched in the starting position. Her balance was thrown off because she was shaking, but she managed to hold her position long enough to hear the starter say, "Swimmers take your marks . . ." And then the sound of the gun blasted.

Reacting to the explosive sound, Lasha threw her body forward into a perfectly streamlined dive. As soon as she felt the cool water cover her body, she forgot everything else. She was doing exactly what she'd trained so hard to do.

In the water Lasha held her streamline. Then she made a wide keyhole-shaped underwater pullout. She added a snap of her wrists at the end to maximize the drive before recovering her arms close to her body into position for her first stroke.

Then Lasha popped out of the water and took

several fast strokes before settling into a good rhythm. For the first length of the four-length race, Lasha swam much stronger than she had in the morning's race. She wanted to hit the pain barrier tonight. She needed to know she'd given her all.

At the first turn, she peeked and saw that she was tied for third place. A fast turn got her off the wall and into another strong pullout. She hit an even faster tempo for the second lap.

The leader of the pack was well ahead of Lasha. The crowd was going crazy for the swimmer in first, the Junior record holder. The energy from the fans spurred Lasha on as she drove her kick harder, making sure to finish in a clean snapping motion.

Another fast turn took Lasha into the third and most difficult lap. *This is when it really starts to hurt,* thought Lasha. But she knew it was also when she had to give that extra something. Lasha broke through the pain barrier as she'd done so many times in practice. Lasha was in The Zone straight through the third lap. She timed her turn perfectly and shot off the wall into the final lap. She had moved up into second place. Now she had to maintain speed through the pain that came back to her for the final lap.

All Lasha could hear was the sound of the fans cheering and the ringing in her ears. She focused on fighting the burning sensations in her tired limbs. By the last few strokes, Lasha was screaming a battle cry inside her head. She took the final lunge into the electronic touchpad. And the race was over.

Totally out of breath, Lasha looked up at the scoreboard. She blinked in disbelief until the swimmer in the next lane reached out to shake Lasha's hand.

"Congratulations. Good swim," said her competitor.

Lasha had come in second place. She had held her position and edged everyone out except the reigning Junior National Champion. She had won the silver medal!

Lasha looked across the pool to Coach Alexia. The Russian woman was smiling and had a fist raised in victory. Lasha looked up to the bleachers. Her mom and dad were hugging, and Ginger was jumping up and down, waving at her. She saw that Pete's smile was huge — and all for her.

A smile crept across Lasha's face as she thought about how the big silver medal would look on her corkboard at home. It meant more than just a swim. Lasha had believed in something big and it had paid off. The rewards went even beyond the shiny medal — a school scholarship, her family's financial burden lifted, higher self-esteem at school, and a new closeness with her brother.

Lasha climbed out of the pool, her limbs shaky and weak from the exertion. But she felt strong and proud on the inside. As she walked down the pool deck toward her coach, Lasha noticed other coaches and swimmers looking at her, nodding with approval.

"Congratulations."

"Nice job."

"Smokin' fast."

It became clear that Lasha was the new kid on the block. Just as Coach Alexia had predicted, she'd blown some of the country's top swimmers out of the water today.

She arrived at her Coach's side.

"Lasha Boyko. Nice swim," said Coach Alexia. Then she looked Lasha right in the eye and added, "This is just the beginning."